UNIVERSUM

Sönke C. Weiss

GUAYAkills

A bloody novella

europabuch

europabuch

www.europabuch.com | info@europabuch.com
ISBN 9791220124386
Erstausgabe: Juni 2022

Gedruckt für Italien von Rotomail Italia
Stampato presso Rotomail Italia S.p.A. - Vignate (MI)

GUAYAkills
A bloody novella by Sönke C. Weiss

For Nina.

Hunting is always preceded by some form of play. The hawk may feint at partridges, harass jackdaws or lapwings, skirmish with crows. Sometimes, without warning, he will suddenly kill. Afterwards he seems baffled by what he has done, and he may leave the kill where it fell and return to it later when he is genuinely hunting. Even when he is hungry, and has killed in anger, he may sit beside his prey for ten to fifteen minutes before starting to feed. In these cases the dead bird is usually unmarked, and the hawk seems to be puzzled by it. He nudges it idly with his bill. When blood flows, he feeds at once.

The Perergine
by J.A. Baker

Part One

1.

You think the future has a cure for the past?

What our heroine thinks as she's floating through downtown Guayaquil, a sprawling shambles of some five million souls.

It's a hot and humid night. But aren't they all, though, in Ecuador's largest and most dangerous city? Hard to imagine a metropolis less hospitable to newcomers.

Our heroine rolls down the window of the taxi and gazes outside. At every turn lurk scammers, thieves and 14-year-old hookers.

Some welcome.

Her eyes also catch sight of neoclassical buildings. Spanish memoirs of a forgotten time.

¡Me importa un huevo!

No.

Absolutely not.

Our heroine doesn't give a fuck. She didn't come here to make this world a better place. Nor did she choose this town for the architecture. Our heroine's not interested in Hop-on Hop-off travelling. Not in that kind of turista.

¡Dios mio!

No.

"New in town, *niña*?" the greasy and middle-aged cabby asks.

¿Niña?

¡Vete a la mierda!

Our heroine doesn't respond. She lights an unfiltered cigarette and smokes it with grand style as the cabby gawks into the rear-view mirror and surveys his passenger while picking a lint ball out of his belly button.

¡De puta madre!

Dark-brown eyes, long neck, an energetic grace, five six, thin and endowed with a nubile body, this girl's a long-limbed beauty. A great vamp figure, like Mona Lisa herself, like a pagan goddess.

Cool as a cucumber and dressed to kill (pun intended and acknowledged) in a sexy, yellow dress our heroine regards her attire much as an army officer views his uniforms: The motive always defines the clothing.

Her wavy brown hair's chin-length, fingernails lacquered a dark blue-green. She's a heroine who looks just like them.

¡Más vale maña que fuerza!

Yeah...

¡De puta madre!

"What's your name, *niña*?" the cabby continues.

¡Niña!

Again!

¡Dame un respiro!

"My name?" our heroine asks. "What's in a name, *amigo*?"

The cabby smirks like a Cheshire cat.

"You okay, *niña*?" he wants to know.

"I'm fine. Okay. But all within a margin of error," our heroine says and continues to stare into the twilight.

The cabby looks bemused and follows suit.

"What we really need is rain. But right now there's no rain in sight," he says as our heroine indulges in her fag.

"Those things will kill ya, *niña*," the cabby says.

"Everything kills ya, *amigo,*" our heroine answers.

It takes a few seconds before the cabby gets the (apparent) joke and laughs. Our heroine smiles faintly and checks out his ugly image in the rear-view mirror. In great detail.

"*Eres muy bonita.* Know anybody in...," the cabby continues to hit on her.

"I've some leads. *Claro,*" she interrupts him.

"Good for you," the cabby answers. "Friends are everything."

"Why's that?" our heroine asks.

The cabby chews over the question for an eternity. (So it seems.) Finally, he says: "When one is helping another, both gain in strength. *Estás muy bonita.*"

Oh, how pretty our heroine is, indeed.

And how indifferently she reacts.

¡Qué cabrón!

"You think the future has a cure for the past?" our heroine reveals what's really on her mind.

The cabby, sharp as a pound of wet liver, can't think of an answer. Besides, he can hardly remember the night before last.

"You can't create the future without knowing what came before it. Don't you agree with me?" our heroine says and repeats herself: "You think the future has a cure for the past?"

¿El pasado?

The cabby ponders somewhat thoroughly, yes painfully as the automobile draws near a red light at the *Parque Seminario* better known as *Parque de Las Iguanas.* Here nobody's in sight.

He stops.

He scratches his rock hard balls and...

...forgets all about our heroine's question.

He simply can't resist her.

He's so *chingada* horny.

¡Me pone malo!

His foul smelling body odor makes our heroine feel nauseated. She can almost taste his sour sweat and imagines how vile and humiliating his cum must be like.

"Little frostbitten, huh? What you need is a fine tune," the cabby says as he zaps through the radio.

Our heroine flicks the cigarette away and rolls up the window.

"What you need, *niña*, what you need is a warm welcome. An oyster loves moisture," the cabby snickers as he unzips his trousers and releases his meaty hard on.

At the same time our heroine pulls a Bond Arms Cowboy Defender Derringer Pistol from her thigh holster and displays the exquisite weapon to the cabby.

"A warm welcome is the easy part, *caballero*," our heroine says.

The cabby grins: *pequeño putilla,* tiny handgun, no big deal! This *niña* is a sitting duck.

¡Carajo!

¡Este es Guayaquil!

"You think something bad's gonna happen, *niña*?" the cabby says as he squeezes his twisted cock.

"I just don't think I'm gonna die in a horizontal position," our heroine answers.

"Now, *niña*, you wanna be really careful with that thing," he says. "Don't wanna have an accident, do you."

"I don't have accidents," our heroine errs.

She points the pistol at the back of the cabby's head, confronting him as if he were a reptile of the lowest order and whispers: "Erick Andres Pena Segale."

The taxi badge, however, reads Antonio de la Cruz.

¡Qué mierda!

Time for a brief but sufficing backstory on the cabby's true identity: Erick Andres Pena Segale aka Antonio de la Cruz was born and raised on Santa Cruz, one of the inhabited Islas Galápagos 563 miles west of continental Ecuador in the Pacific Ocean.

His father was a fisherman who had taught his mother how a man must be treated; the typical Ecuadorian approach to an everlasting marriage now and then: put up and shut up. A very clear life for the young Erick Andres Pena Segale aka Antonio de la Cruz.

In 1977, despite his unimpressive yet characteristic genetic material common for his people on the islands, mixed descendants of Spanish colonists and natives who are champions in the art of unselective inbreeding, he arrived in Guayaquil with a scholarship for the Colegio Alemán Humboldt.

Abbreviation: CAH.

Motto: *La solidaridad es y fue siempre un valor fundaméntale.*

In other words: sweet alms-giving for the bitterly underprivileged.

Erick Andres Pena Segale aka Antonio de la Cruz lived with his uncle who ran a taxi business. Smoked herb and jerked off. Jerked off and smoked herb. Did poorly in school. Couldn't find his ass with two hands and a road map. Not the finest specimen for natural selection. Finished last in his class of 1986. Became a cab driver. What the fuck else! All crooks anyway.

Erick Andres Pena Segale aka Antonio de la Cruz too got himself in trouble with the law. Murder, armed robbery, kidnapping, sexual assault. You name it. He did it.

His prey: tourists.

His incentive: *Más vale llegar a tiempo que en convidado.*

Id est: It's better to arrive at the right moment than to be invited.

Changed his name. Kept the job.

¡Madre mia!

¡Este es Guayaquil!

¡Este es Ecuador!

Survival of the fittest.

Not the brightest.

End of story.

"How...," Erick Andres Pena Segale aka Antonio de la Cruz begins to ask our heroine as their eyes lock in the rear-view mirror.

He's met by icy glares.

Our heroine looks like the cat that finally got the cream.

"*Tienes ojos muy bonitos,*" Erick Andres Pena Segale aka Antonio de la Cruz gives our heroine a last compliment.

¡Cierra el pico!

"You wanna sanctify yourself, Erick Andres Pena Segale?" our heroine says. "There's no time but the present. But those who cannot remember the past, are condemned to repeat it."

Silencio.

Silencio absoluto.

Silencio muerto.

Dead silence.

Because it hits him like a punch in the face. That she's the one.

¡Jodida!

Fucking A...

Though our heroine offers him a second chance, Erick Andres Pena Segale aka Antonio de la Cruz doesn't come clean. He's several vertebrae short of a backbone. Instead, his impulse is to escape. But the *cobarde* doesn't dare!

"I remember you now, *niña*," he says instead. "I'm not guilty. I'm just a chauffeur. I'm nobody."

Our heroine cocks the gun...

"When the treasure chest is open, even the just man sins. Will this last long? *Scheiße*," Erick Andres Pena Segale aka Antonio de la Cruz utters the only word he remembers from his German classes.

...and blows his fucking brains out.

Finito.

Erick Andres Pena Segale's aka Antonio de la Cruz's left hand releases his imprisoned manhood, his right hand remains on the radio dial. It's covered with blood and cerebral cortex. He's very dead but he's also found a very fine tune. On Radio Tropicana. 96.5 fm.

Ecuador's most famous radio personality, Alejandro Mateo Torres Estrada, who our heroine shall visit soon, presents the song *Adoracion.*

She hears the velvety voice of Enrique Ibáñez Mora: "*Soñé ser tuyo y en mi efántenerte prese en mis brazos para siempre mia; pero nunca soñé que he de perderte que otro mortal la dicha soureia.*"

With tears running down her face our heroine grabs her suitcase and exits the yellow cab into the darkness as a six foot iguana sluggishly climbs into the taxi.

While the slow and melancholic Ecuadorian pasillo fills the empty Agosto Avenue, the animal devours what's left of Erick Andres Pena Segale's aka Antonio de la Cruz's pathetic head.

Time passes and does not forgive...

2.

On Friday, April 1, 2016, a young, nameless woman out of nowhere arrives in Santiago de Guayaquil, Ecuador. No one knows who she is, or why she came, or what makes her do the ghastly things she does. They only know she has a terrifying beauty and a killer IQ. And that each time she appears, a man dies - horribly! Cabby Erick Andres Pena Segale aka Antonio de la Cruz is only her first victim.

One week later. Friday, April 8, 2016. The Sheraton Guayaquil Hotel. Plaza del Sol. A suite on the top floor. Two champagne glasses clink together.

"From today on, *mi amigo, fidelidad, fidelidad,*" Alejandro Mateo Torres Estrada proudly announces his new way of life to his best man who responds at once: "Are you serious?"

¡Por dios!

Alejandro Mateo Torres Estrada - a different man?

"Always try to do something that's a little beyond your reach," the acclaimed and leading radio host declares.

His friend knows him better though: "Alejandro Mateo Torres Estrada, you can resist everything. Except *tentación*!"

They laugh and sip Dom Perignon, and here's what's important to know about Alejandro Mateo Torres Estrada:

Only child.

Father's a businessman.

Mother's a lawyer.

Like Erick Andres Pena Segale aka Antonio de la Cruz was formed at the CAH. Its official mission reads as follows: *respeto y tolerancia.* Well...

Graduated in 1986. Unlike Erick Andres Pena Segale aka Antonio de la Cruz best of his class. Subsequently one year at the Humboldt University of Berlin in former Westdeutschland where he not only perfected his Teuton language skills but also learned to master other oral techniques on his fellow female classmates with such exotic-sounding and downright seductive names as Claudia, Petra and Katja. No wonder Alejandro Mateo Torres Estrada loved the Old World.

Then undergraduate work at the University of Miami, Florida, USofA. (Quote Alejandro Mateo Torres Estrada: "United States of Assholes!") Double major in journalism and marketing. (Quote Alejandro Mateo Torres Estrada: "I'll show these gringos what a greaser can do.") Pulled a 4.0. But no extracurricular, no hook-up activities. Needless to say that he loathed the Land of Liberty. (Quote Alejandro Mateo Torres Estrada: "*Agua que no has de beber, déjala correr.*") In other words: all cock no action. *Nada.* Alas Alejandro Mateo Torres Estrada did not hit it off with the all-American girl(s). Despite his delicious appearance. Big white even teeth and all.

A wetback is a wetback is a wetback is a wetback. (Sorry, Gertrude Stein.) But things are what they are in the Sunshine State.

Mexico?

Ecuador?

Who gives a fuck?

Back home in Ecuador, quick career in the media circus thanks to his father's well-oiled machine with each piece of human resource doing the job it should do and even quicker in countless girl's panties thanks to his unusual good looks.

Sunday nights visits to Salinas or 18th street (*Zona de Tolerancia*) where blooming girls from neighboring Colombia or the Esmeraldas province in northwest Ecuador charge $8 a lay (sexually transmitted diseases included) are an important and consistent part of his weekly recreational program that his old man introduced him to: *Amor con amor se paga; y lo* demás *con dinero.* Which basically means: money makes the world go round. Not love. Not love.

But you gotta love Guayaquil.

Gotta love your *mujer de la vida* - your working girls who can loosen the cap of a two liter coke bottle with their vagina. (Quote Alejandro Mateo Torres Estrada: "A tight pussy is worth its weight in gold to any man.")

Presently in his late forties but still dashingly-handsome as his *chicas* say and a true champion in "G-spotting" as Alejandro Mateo Torres Estrada claims, it's finally time to get married, it's at last time for his own family.

Papá dijo...

Today's the day.

The religious blessing has already been given.

Alejandro Mateo Torres Estrada is getting ready for his wedding reception.

His best man keeps him company. They are full of admiration for each other. *Mejores amigos.* Both suited up in midnight blue tuxedos.

Real bosom buddies.

Real swingers.

But not both ways.

¡Este es Guayaquil!

However...

"You think sinners are as deserving of the good things in life as saints?" Alejandro Mateo Torres Estrada asks.

"Well," his best man answers, "boys are born with privileges girls don't even take into account."

"You're right. Girls are born with beautiful gifts and burdens," Alejandro Mateo Torres Estrada says.

"They're born to be trained," his best man counters.

"They're born to be perfect," Alejandro Mateo Torres Estrada snaps back.

"They're born to weep," his best man returns.

"And to be - ours," Alejandro Mateo Torres Estrada salutes.

"That's why tradition will never let us down," his best man acknowledges.

"A toast!" Alejandro Mateo Torres Estrada demands.

"A toast!" his best man insists.

"To tradition!" Alejandro Mateo Torres Estrada proclaims.

"What else is there?" his best man jubilates.

The two *hombres* laugh boisterously, toast and drink as Alejandro Mateo Torres Estrada continues getting dressed. He studies himself in the mirror.

"A reflection can be so misleading," he says unexpectedly.

The best man notices Alejandro Mateo Torres Estrada's sudden lack of motivation. He's perplexed by his friend's unenthusiastic attitude.

"You've nothing to worry about, *mi amigo,*" he says. "Look, you anchor the most distinguished program on Radio Tropicana. You've the country at your feet. Everything you touch turns to gold. Your work has paid off. Nobody, *mi amigo,* nobody can take your life away from you. Not even marriage."

Alejandro Mateo Torres Estrada continues to check out his facial features - and then his permanent.

"*Scheiße,*" he shouts his favorite German word.

"C'mon. What's the matter? You're not at peace with your hair?" the best man notices.

Alejandro Mateo Torres Estrada begins to fix it. His actions show evidence of feverish activity and haste. Until his best man steps forward and interrupts him.

"Easy, *mi amigo,* you look great," he says.

"Are you sure?" Alejandro Mateo Torres Estrada asks.

"Why does a husband always remind me of someone pregnant with hemming and hawing?" the best man laughs and begins to work on Alejandro Mateo Torres Estrada's hairdo who does make an attempt to snap out of his mood. He can't, though.

Thinking about...

¿Niña?

"Maybe he gets nostalgic when he speaks to a bachelor," his best man continues and giggles.

...a shadow of his past.

¡Niña!

"Or maybe he realizes that he was wrong," Alejandro Mateo Torres Estrada continues.

"Wrong about what?" his best man asks.

"Things," Alejandro Mateo Torres Estrada says after a few seconds.

"I understand," his best man answers. "But if you don't go around telling everybody how wrong you were nobody will know."

He steps back and looks at Alejandro Mateo Torres Estrada's head. He likes what he sees, what he has done to Alejandro Mateo Torres Estrada's hair, looking all bouffant now.

"We've had sweet times together," Alejandro Mateo Torres Estrada changes the subject. "Very sweet times."

He approaches his best man and takes his hands.

"Our days were *tranquilo,*" the best man replies and kisses Alejandro Mateo Torres Estrada's hands.

"Most in-laws would have a different opinion," Alejandro Mateo Torres Estrada whispers.

The men chuckle.

"It's good to have a silent friend, *mi amigo,*" the best friend sighs.

"If women didn't talk who would do all the talking?" Alejandro Mateo Torres Estrada asks *retórico* and begins to pet his best man's hands.

"You might be a giant of a man. You may begin to grow grey hair. You may be bold and toothless with age. But if you're unmarried, you're nothing," the best man affirms.

"Thank you. Thank you. Thank you," Alejandro Mateo Torres Estrada says and looks into his best man's eyes.

Deep.

Too deep?

Perhaps.

"You're welcome, *mi amigo.* You're welcome," he answers while almost shedding tears reminiscing on their friendship thinking: *'Soy todo tuyo.'* I am yours. But he doesn't say it. Instead, the best man takes his mobile phone out of his back pocket and quickly shoots a selfie of them. While they toast. One last time. Both dreaming:

'Quiero envejecer contigo' I wanna grow old with you. *Pero...*

¡Este es Guayaquil!

"Ready?" Alejandro Mateo Torres Estrada's best man finally asks.

"Only just...," Alejandro Mateo Torres Estrada answers and goes to the bathroom where he swiftly does a line of blow... as his best man looks out of the window into the sky.

He's captivated by the view. Although there're no stars to be seen, no moon in sight. Nothing but obscurity.

"In this hour the atmosphere takes on an imprisoned harshness," he says to himself while posting the selfie on Facebook.

"What'd you say?" his best friends asks as he's coming back from the loo buttoning his pants and wiping his nose.

"Nothing, really," the best man replies and stuffs the mobile phone in his back pocket. "Shall we go?"

"You bet, *mi amigo,* we shall go," Alejandro Mateo Torres Estrada agrees.

The men embrace.

Long.

Too long.

Perhaps.

El amor es ciego, pero los vecinos no.

¡Este es...!

Alejandro Mateo Torres Estrada's about to say something, but he stammers instead and leaves the suite.

His best man views him distractedly and tails him to the lift which drops as smooth as butter. Embedded by elevator music, an instrumental arrangement of *Adoracion,* Alejandro Mateo Torres Estrada cleans his fingernails with his teeth as his best man checks his mobile phone for messages. Until...

... the lift stops.

The door opens.

And they're greeted by tremendous applause.

The best man looks at Alejandro Mateo Torres Estrada and nods.

Alejandro Mateo Torres Estrada nods back.

Together they beam at the wedding guests.

¡Bueno!

Almost at the same time...

...a Shady Lady, a chopper style bike custom designed *para chicas guay* arrives at the main entrance of the Sheraton Guayaquil Hotel. (Okay, she does not so much arrive, she's floating into the entrance.)

Our heroine, the girl with the nubile body and the energetic grace, is riding the motorcycle. Her hair's long and blond. She's dressed in a tight, red dress, revealing more than just her knees, and shiny red leather boots. A red silk scarf covers her bare shoulders. (Gasp!) An Aphrodite. She's a supernova who digs the grand entrance. She plummets into it. She's a show with no intermission. Her curtain is always rising. Her sense of play is serious.

Our heroine stops, glides off the hog, her muscles flexing as she pulls down her dress, throws the keys to the dumbfounded valet (gasp! gasp!) and, without saying a word, strides into the elegant lobby.

Her body language resembles a model strolling through a clothing store. (Does anyone else besides the writer of this novella have a crush on our nameless heroine, yet?) Hotel guests stare at her. Steadfast our heroine continues until she reaches Alejandro Mateo Torres Estrada's swanky wedding reception.

¡Caramba!

It has to be done...

"It had to be done," Alejandro Mateo Torres Estrada's best man says full of pride and reaches out grabbing his shoulder.

¡Es hora de fiesta!

The two men linger in the middle of a few hundred wedding guests. Rose petals cover the floor. A young girl carries a bible. Everybody expresses festive action and great joy. Everybody seems to feel that everything's seems to be all right.

¡Vaya una fiesta!

People are happy and talk a lot!

People are hungry and eat a lot!

People are thirsty and drink a lot!

Waiters rush by. With enormous plates of food: *Ceviche. Cevichochos. Empanadas. Pan de Yuca. Pinchos. Guatitas. Seco de Chivo. Seco de Pollo* and, of course, *Cuy* - guinea pig. (To-go baggies already waiting.) The guests wash *todo* down with *Aguardiente* and *Canelazo.*

An enormous wedding cake is waiting to be cut. Countless bottles of Johnny Walker Red Label are impatient to be drunk.

Mamá, soy demente, an experimental rock band, is waiting in the wings. (Alejandro Mateo Torres Estrada insisted! After all, he considers himself to be a modern man.)

His bride, nice-looking but nothing to write home about, arrives and whispers something in his ear.

Alejandro Mateo Torres Estrada grins. He's in a chipper and frivolous mood now.

Gracias al alcohol...

...and a few more lines of fine Colombian bam-bam.

"I can't wait, *cariño,*" he tells her.

She kisses Alejandro Mateo Torres Estrada's cheek and leaves while his best man eyes our heroine. She waits several feet away from them and - grins.

Frozen to statuesque stillness.

The Mecca and Medina of every man.

Goddamn lil Mama.

Need to get her over to my crib and do that night thang.

What a bait!

"Adventure is on its way," the best man imagines.

"I had to marry a virgin", Alejandro Mateo Torres Estrada misunderstands. "I loathe strife."

"No, *mi amigo,*" his best man opposes and points at our heroine. "You know her?"

Straightaway Alejandro Mateo Torres Estrada falls in love with our heroine. He stares at her as if she was the burning bush. Our heroine continues to smirk at the two men.

"I sure don't," Alejandro Mateo Torres Estrada tells his best man. "But at times we're in heaven for a minute. She's sure something a man can get his teeth into."

"You know what they say," his best man disclosures.

Alejandro Mateo Torres Estrada can't but stare at the unknown woman.

"Some dinners bite back," his best man continues.

Alejandro Mateo Torres Estrada gleams with anticipation and begins hopping from foot to foot.

"I haven't had a good night's sleep since last week, and I'm looking forward to one tonight," his best man says as he makes his move. "*Se sentó en la mesa y atacó la cena.*"

And...

...walks over to our heroine as Alejandro Mateo Torres Estrada observes the scene. He's restless. He wants to be part of the game, but the train has passed. He imagines his best friend and... flutters his eyes at our heroine while his bride returns. She remarks that her newlywed husband appears distracted.

"You okay, *mi amor?*" she asks.

Alejandro Mateo Torres Estrada has half a mind to talk to her right now. But he recalls that she is his wife.

¡Maldito!

"Of course, *mi amor,*" he answers, kissing his bride who now sees our heroine in the distance talking to her spouse's best man.

"He's a lucky guy," she says.

"No, *mi amor,* I'm the lucky guy," Alejandro Mateo Torres Estrada lies.

His *esposa* smiles happily and leaves again to join the party, while Alejandro Mateo Torres Estrada stares at our heroine. She's heavily seducing his best man.

¡Eso es suficiente!

Alejandro Mateo Torres Estrada decides to join them and is warmly but silently welcomed by his best man and our heroine. The three look at each other.

Alejandro Mateo Torres Estrada's immersed by our heroine's riveting aura. After a while his best man begins to speak.

"*¿Quieres algo de tomar?*" he asks our heroine who nods while staring deeply into Alejandro Mateo Torres Estrada's eyes.

His best man leaves for the bar acknowledging that this pursuit of happiness did feel a bit crowded. Alejandro Mateo Torres Estrada smiles at our heroine. He's awestruck by her soft yet sizzling eyes.

"Oh, how hard it is to make a decision," our heroine says. "So many men to choose from, which one should I take?"

Oh, what a method-actor she is...

Alejandro Mateo Torres Estrada's speechless.

¡La bruja!

"Your bride's an angel," our heroine promptly advances the conversation.

Alejandro Mateo Torres Estrada peeks at his better half who jokes around with her seven bridesmaids.

"Yes," he says, "one day you might be a bride too and an angel. Would that make you happy?"

Our heroine closes her eyes, and for a split second...

"What's your name?" he asks her.

"Superwoman," she answers quickly getting back into the game.

Alejandro Mateo Torres Estrada grins flirtatiously.

The philanderer in him is back.

Fuck *fidelidad*!

The courtesan in her has won.

Alejandro Mateo Torres Estrada takes the hook.

"Well, hello, Superwoman. I'm the Dark Knight," he says. "What would your superpower be?"

"Melting people with love," our heroine answers.

"You came to the right place," Alejandro Mateo Torres Estrada parries.

Our heroine takes his hand.

"My mind's empty. My body's radiant," she says. "You wanna take me somewhere more appropriate, somewhere more deserved and just? You wanna show me heaven? What's your fantasy?"

Alejandro Mateo Torres Estrada shrugs. His eyes search for his bride who's nowhere to be seen.

"What's your fantasy?" he asks innocently.

"Loving. Living. Everything," our heroine answers.

"Just like me," Alejandro Mateo Torres Estrada reports.

"To share a fantasy is another fantasy," our heroine teases him.

"I think...," he begins.

"...you can trust your instincts, but you still need to know," our heroine finishes Alejandro Mateo Torres Estrada's sentence.

"I do. I do need to know," he says.

"Convince me," our heroine laughs. "Let's be spontaneous. Certain things are better done in a rush!"

"I'm not sure...," Alejandro Mateo Torres Estrada stumbles...

...and our heroine backs off.

She releases his hand and says: "I've never acted inappropriately with anyone. I apologize."

Alejandro Mateo Torres Estrada plays it cool.

"I've nothing to object to in what you're saying. I've my reasons", he says.

"The terrible thing is," our heroine responds as she glares into Alejandro Mateo Torres Estrada's eyes, "the terrible thing is that everyone has his reasons."

Alejandro Mateo Torres Estrada contemplates, calculates, plans and decides. Like his best man said, he can resist everything.

Except *la tentación.*

"Follow me," he orders taking again possession of the auspicious hand.

¡El tonto!

Without attracting attention, Alejandro Mateo Torres Estrada and our heroine leave the wedding reception.

His best man returns with a scotch on the rocks. He watches as Alejandro Mateo Torres Estrada and our heroine walk out.

"A small talk may cause a big disaster," he says to himself as Alejandro Mateo Torres Estrada and our heroine already stand in the lift.

Again ambient music.

Again *Adoracion.*

Alejandro Mateo Torres Estrada pushes a button. The lift ascends sleek as silk as he begins to tinker with his hair.

"Are you fearless?" our heroine asks.

Alejandro Mateo Torres Estrada faces her and cannot help but register an ongoing appreciation of her beauty.

"Cause God hates a coward. Mightily," our heroine continues.

Alejandro Mateo Torres Estrada clears his throat as he looks sternly at our heroine.

"I'm...," he begins.

"Hush," our heroine interrupts him. "Think twice before burdening a woman with a secret. Love and desire are two different things; that not everything you love is desired, nor everything that is desired is loved."

Our heroine presses herself against Alejandro Mateo Torres Estrada.

"If you dig it - it's yours," she says. "Don't you think I'm gorgeously fertile?"

Alejandro Mateo Torres Estrada begins to perspire.

The lift stops.

The door opens.

Our heroine exits first.

Alejandro Mateo Torres Estrada follows her assuming a confidential pose as they reach the hotel roof where...

...he appears clearly impatient looking at his watch. The pricey timepiece on his wrist, an Oyster Perpetual Day-Date II Rolex, of course, reads 8.15 P.M.

It's still hot and humid.

Indeed, oppressively hot and humid and pitch-dark.

Our heroine stares into the starless sky.

"Stars don't care what you wish for," she renders.

"I know what I wish for," Alejandro Mateo Torres Estrada implies as he's divesting himself of his tuxedo jacket.

"How do you feel?" our heroine asks him.

"I feel awesome. Whatever that is," he answers, flinging his jacket on the ground.

¡El chulo!

Suddenly our heroine does see a star. It's a shooting star. She follows it with her finger and says: "A shooting star never hit anyone."

"Have we met before?" Alejandro Mateo Torres Estrada asks.

"We're all in the gutter, but some of us are looking at the stars. You tell me," our heroine suggests.

Alejandro Mateo Torres Estrada reflects. He gives our heroine an aching look as she moves closer to the edge of the roof while feeling her breasts with her fingertips.

"My bosom conceals two silver coins. He who touches them becomes a saint," she says.

Alejandro Mateo Torres Estrada approaches our heroine. He glances over the edge - carefully.

"Oh wow, oh wow, oh wow," he yaks and hastily moves backwards.

"You better be careful, *niña!*" Alejandro Mateo Torres Estrada rushes.

¿Niña?

¡Niña!

"Say what you like to me, a woman does as she pleases," our heroine shouts.

Alejandro Mateo Torres Estrada gets jittery.

"What do you wanna hear?" he flaps.

"Already in the 1930s, an astrophysicist suggested that the brightly shining stars represented only a part of the cosmic whole. There must also be 'dark matter', unseen but revealed indirectly by the effects of gravity. So, either Einstein is wrong about gravity, or gravitational pull from vast amounts of something invisible is holding the stars together. Dark matter! Who wants to take a wife, and who seeks a husband? That's what I wanna hear," our heroine says.

Alejandro Mateo Torres Estrada doesn't understand.

"Is this a joke?" he asks.

¡Qué tonta eres!

Our heroine desperately tries not to laugh. She takes off her scarf and throws one end of it to Alejandro Mateo Torres Estrada. He catches it. Our heroine pulls him more and more towards her.

"You think I'm joking?" she asks.

"That's crazy," Alejandro Mateo Torres Estrada gabs. "You're crazy!"

"I'm not crazy," our heroine answers. "Cruelty's crazy!"

Alejandro Mateo Torres Estrada, close to the edge of the roof, peeks into the void.

"Come again?" he says.

"Just look straight into my eyes," our heroine says.

Alejandro Mateo Torres Estrada follows her order.

"It's easy to fool the eye. It's hard to fool the heart," she claims.

Our heroine's eyes sparkle. Suddenly she wheels around him. Akin to a cat of prey. Alejandro Mateo Torres Estrada now stands right on the edge and has a hard time keeping his balance.

"Look at me, Alejandro Mateo Torres Estrada," our heroine demands.

And...

...Alejandro Mateo Torres Estrada freezes.

"How...," he begins.

"We've met before. If I cried out, would you hear me? I'm still the one who knelt before you," our heroine explains.

Alejandro Mateo Torres Estrada recognizes our heroine.

¡Mierda!

His eyes reflect panic and - shame. Similar to the cabby's eyes a week earlier.

"You're the fucking wife, the bloody *niña*," Alejandro Mateo Torres Estrada screams leaning dangerously over the edge.

"Tell me what you saw, Alejandro Mateo Torres Estrada," our heroine demands. "Give me peace of mind."

But Alejandro Mateo Torres Estrada, *el ablanda-higos*, keeps quiet and blows his second chance just like Erick Andres Pena Segale aka Antonio de la Cruz before him.

"The descent to hell is the same from every place. Every secret is eventually revealed," our heroine says and - lets go of the scarf...

"Wait a minute," Alejandro Mateo Torres Estrada begs.

...allowing him to fall to his death while back at the wedding reception the guests have finally begun to dance.

Alejandro Mateo Torres Estrada's best man waits in front of a window and punches a number in his mobile phone as Alejandro Mateo Torres Estrada drops out of the sky behind him.

¡Mierda!

Unnoticed, a flagpole skewers him like a shesh kebab.

¡Hostia!

Alejandro Mateo Torres Estrada's brother in spirit begins to shimmy to *Mamá, soy demente* playing *Satanas en Sotanas...*

...whilst our heroine exits the Sheraton Guayaquil Hotel. She looks like someone leaving a courtroom in victory.

Our heroine plucks the keys to her Shady Lady out of the valet's key box and mounts the bike. At the same time her silk scarf comes flying down towards her. She grabs it and throws it around her neck.

At that instant, from somewhere out near the back of the hotel, Alejandro Mateo Torres Estrada's brand-new widow screams heartbreakingly.

The wedding party comes to an abrupt end as our heroine purrs off.

¡Adiós!

¡Bienvenida!

Only a few believers are present in the Santa Ana Hill Chapel located in the picturesque *barrio* of *Las Peñas.*

The men wear kippahs and are scattered to the four winds. Rabbi Nepomuk Glass hauls himself up the altar.

Nepomuk is in his late eighties, regally wrinkled and in superb mental condition. He's diligent about his routines. Moving his legs, however, takes the wind out of him. His knees squeak, crack and pop like a xylophone band.

Nepomuk, frowning and uncomfortable, is in severe pain. He turns around and begins to address the attendees...

...and in a flash it's as if he's just shed twenty years. Nepomuk speaks Spanish with a thick German accent.

"In each of us there's another whom we do not know," he begins as our nameless heroine, the girl with the mind-blowing beauty and the killer IQ, enters the chapel. She's notably stripped down, an unbleached appearance.

Dressed all in grey, makeup-free with mud-puddle hair. Our heroine has no eyes for the interior of the place. Old paintings that make reference to the crucifixion and death of Jesus Christ. Or the nineteen stained glass windows. Fourteen of them represent... But as we know, our heroine didn't come here for this kind *of turista.* She places herself in the last row and listens to what Nepomuk has to say to the congregation.

"Your heights are your own mountain which belongs to you and you alone," he continues.

"Then you are an individual and live your very own life. But how can we know ourselves by ourselves? Souls need intimate connection, not only to individuate, but simply to live. For this we need relationships of the profoundest kind through which we can realize ourselves, where self-revelation is possible, where interest in and love for the soul is paramount. Love is the burning point of life, and since all life is sorrowful, so is love. The stronger the love, the more the pain. But love bears all things. Love itself is pain, you might say - the pain of being truly alive."

Silence.

Except the noise of one man snoring. He's fallen asleep. Nepomuk coughs slightly.

"No one lives his life," he goes on getting more and more passionate. "We're disguised by childhood. Randomly put together from voices and worries and little pleasures. We come of age as masks. Our true face never speaks. Somewhere there must be storehouses where all these lives are laid away like suits of armor or clothes hanging limply on the walls. Maybe all paths lead there, to the repository of unlived things."

Silence.

Nepomuk blows out the candles of the menorah, the seven-branched candelabrum normally used in the Temple.

Nobody moves.

Nepomuk looks at his people and...

"You may go home now. Go home and be your wonderful selves", he says.

¡Joder!

The men shuffle out of the chapel as Nepomuk stuffs the sconce in his knapsack. He gradually descends from the altar. Step by step he walks to the entrance of the sanctuary. He looks like someone walking on the moon.

Eventually he notices our heroine who hasn't left yet. Nepomuk approaches her. He doesn't get too close, though.

"The service was a great success," he says. "But the audience was a disaster."

Our heroine looks puzzled. A rabbi in a Catholic church? Moreover, she's never seen a real one before. A rabbi!

¡Que demonios...!

"I'm rabbi Nepomuk Glass," Nepomuk introduces himself. "Everybody calls me Nepo. Shalom."

Our heroine doesn't respond.

¡Por dios!

"The church lets us use this space. We are not so many," Nepomuk continues. "Actually, we were never so many."

Our heroine and Nepomuk look at each other.

In silence.

"You're welcome to join us. If you like. We meet on Friday evenings and Saturday mornings," Nepomuk invites our heroine and continues to leave.

"Looking good is nothing compared with the pleasure of still being able to put one foot in front of the other and move", he says.

Our heroine watches Nepomuk with a puzzled expression, slightly confused by his cynicism mixed with sobriety, not knowing that their paths will cross again soon, that his story will become hers and hers his and that they will forge a bond for eternity, a bond not even God could untie. Ever.

"I'm a slow walker," he says as he exits the chapel, "but I never walk back."

Our heroine remains behind.

Solo...

...as back in the Sheraton Guayaquil Hotel Captain Luis Fernando Sanchez Zamora from the Policía Nacional del Ecuador scrutinizes the speared Alejandro Mateo Torres Estrada whose dead body is wrapped in a blue and white Guayaquil flag looking like a tortilla oozing salsa.

¡Es la hora!

Time's up, Alejandro Mateo Torres Estrada, and here's what we need to know about Captain Sanchez Zamora: Like the victim and the victim before, he's in his late forties. His hardened bad temper shakes buildings. His cheerier moods on the other hand melt ice. Captain Sanchez Zamora wears Coke-bottle-thick glasses and looks like a cross between Boris Karloff and Harvey Weinstein with an ironic eyebrow as perfected by Marlene Dietrich. His eyes also spot zeitgeist long before it comes over the hill. Which is why a city full of incandescent fabulousness pivots around a man who looks like nothing so much as a bean-bag chair with legs.

Exactamente.

The hotel manager approaches him from behind as Captain Sanchez Zamora's eating a large piece of Alejandro Mateo Torres Estrada's wedding cake.

Apropos bean-bag chair with legs. There's one more detail concerning Captain Sanchez Zamora's nature. He eats all the time and packs at least forty extra pounds on his five six frame because he can't say no to all the delicious things coming his way. That's why his stomach hangs over his belt buckle holder in which a Little Joe Five Shot Revolver is embedded.

¡El bastardo!

"Excuse me, *Señor*. This is a crime scene," the hotel manager charges as Captain Sanchez Zamora continues to feed himself and doesn't react.

"*Señor*!" the hotel manager continues. "Please leave. And who are you anyway?"

Captain Sanchez Zamora turns around and demonstrates his best MD eyebrow ever.

"I own one single suit that I'm wearing right now and in the last 25 years," he growls. "I've never had another suit. And the shoes that I'm wearing I've been wearing for three years and they're my only pair of shoes. I need to replace them because they're starting to come apart."

And after a perfect pause Captain Sanchez Zamora adds: "I'm God's middle finger. Who the fuck are you?"

"Show some decency. The man is dead," the hotel manager says as he looks at the plate in Captain Sanchez Zamora's fleshy hand.

¡Estás loco!

Captain Sanchez Zamora approaches the hotel manager. He examines him with stupefied indignation and rage.

"Death is my daily bread. Death is my good morning and good night. Tell me, you *gilipollas*, where have all the flowers gone?" he says as Lieutenant Gino Leandro Ortega Revelo interrupts him.

"Captain Sanchez Zamora is l- l- l-eading the investigation", he says. "I'm L- L- L-ieutenant Ortega Revelo."

Lieutenant Gino Leandro Ortega Revelo is in his early twenties, has a cleft lip and stutters. He's very eager to please. Especially his boss, Captain Sanchez Zamora, who treats him to the carrot or stick method because the truth is: Lieutenant Ortega Revelo resembles a man who can't walk and chew gum at the same time.

But he's a decent cop who performs his job by the book. Even though the government at times neglects to pay its civil servants, including the Policía Nacional del Ecuador, for months in a row. Contrary to his comrades who are masters of corruption, extortion, bribery, theft, burglary, stealing items from crime scenes (so-called shakedowns), withholding evidence (better known as fixing, perjury, internal payoffs, planting of evidence what insiders call frame ups) and of course the beloved cancelling of traffic tickets as a favor to friends and loved ones.

A code of silence amongst the policemen prevents all of the above fun activities from coming to light. In other words: in Guayaquil one becomes a police officer in order to fuck other people up. Case closed.

¡Este es...!

"You m- m- m-ay have heard of Captain Sanchez Zamora", Lieutenant Ortega Revolo says to the hotel manager with a slight smirk.

"I have. Of course. I'm sorry," the hotel manager apologizes.

¡Afortunado!

Lucky him, because Captain Sanchez Zamora's reputation is legendary all over the country. He stares at the hotel manager as the man begins to weasel: "I'm so very sorry, *Señor.* Profoundly sorry, *Señor.* I'm new to the city. Your city. But I've heard of you. Of course. I'm deeply sorry."

Captain Sanchez Zamora delights in the moment.

"Apology accepted and enjoyed," he finally says. "Man's skin is too thin for this world. I think, you can't let your skin get too thick."

"We'll q- q- q-uestion you later. Thank you very m- m- m-uch," Lieutenant Ortega Revelo says to the hotel manager as Captain Sanchez Zamora licks his fingers.

¡Lárgate!

The hotel manager leaves in a rush. Lieutenant Ortega Revelo beholds the deceased Alejandro Mateo Torres Estrada and looks nauseated.

"Before the w- w- w-edding night. That's deeply bizarre and deeply creepy. Can't wait to tell my f- f- fiancee about this one," he says and adds quickly: "Am I a- a- a-llowed to tell her, *patron*?"

"You try the cake?" Captain Sanchez Zamora asks.

Lieutenant Ortega Revelo looks at the empty plate.

"It's divine," Captain Sanchez Zamora continues. "Must be gluten-free."

He eyes a waitress and waves her over.

"*Hola, niña,*" he shouts.

The waitress arrives quickly. Captain Sanchez Zamora points at the empty plate.

"I've had a few but too few to mention," he whispers.

The waitress nods, takes the plate and leaves.

"Are you a good chef, Lieutenant?" Captain Sanchez Zamora asks.

Lieutenant Ortega Revelo ponders.

"You know that the best chefs in the world are men, don't you?" Captain Sanchez Zamora continues as he pulls a Swiss Army knife out of his pocket.

It features a toothpick. He uses it to clean his teeth. Lieutenant Ortega Revelo appears to be very interested in the knife.

"I d- d- d-idn't know that, *patron*,", he says.

"It's a fact," Captain Sanchez Zamora explains, "that ladies can't stand what? They can't stand the heat. Men take cooking more seriously. I'm not saying women can't be top chefs. And yet, as a man, I don't want to roll back to the bad old days. In less enlightened times, men tended to associate cooking with what? With women, with the ceremonial exception of outdoor grilling. How is it that these hunters have suddenly turned into gatherers? Don't they know that they're going against the rules of basic evolutionary psychology? Most offensively, it also negates centuries of cooking by women. Can we honestly contend that all culinary artistry was accomplished by men who went against their biological destinies? You know, Lieutenant, there are also a lot of men who can't hack it in the kitchen, yes. But I have what? I have high hopes that things are changing."

Captain Sanchez Zamora slides the toothpick back into the knife and stuffs the instrument into his pocket. Lieutenant Ortego Revelo's eyes follow the tool/weapon. Depending on...

"Cute," he asks stoically, "what's it m- m- m-ade of?"

"Memories, Lieutenant," Captain Sanchez Zamora replies. "It's made of nifty memories."

The waitress arrives with a new piece of wedding cake. She hands the plate to Captain Sanchez Zamora.

"Thank you, *niña*," he says with a smile.

The waitress grins back.

"It is gluten-free, isn't it?" Captain Sanchez Zamora asks her.

"I don't know, *Señor*," she answers.

"I don't know, *Señor*?" Captain Sanchez Zamora repeats.

"No," she says.

"I don't know, Captain," Captain Sanchez Zamora corrects her.

The waitress begins to shiver. Her friendliness vanishes at once.

"I don't know, Captain," she mutters and ducks out as Captain Sanchez Zamora offers the plate to Lieutenant Ortego Revelo.

"Anger of the mind is poison to the soul. You sure you don't wanna bite?" Captain Sanchez Zamora says.

Lieutenant Ortego Revelo shakes his head and looks at his notes.

"According to our witness the d- d- d-eceased...," Lieutenant Ortego Revelo begins.

"His name was Alejandro Mateo Torres Estrada," Captain Sanchez Zamora says.

"I'm s- s- s-orry?" Lieutenant Ortego Revelo asks.

"Alejandro Mateo Torres Estrada," Captain Sanchez Zamora repeats.

"You just arrived. Did you talk to a- a- a-nybody? You kn- kn- kn-ew him?" Lieutenant Ortego Revelo asks.

"No and yes. I did know him," Captain Sanchez Zamora replies.

"How?" Lieutenant Ortega Revelo asks.

"We used to work together. Capacity building. Everything we loved we had to defend. Even in school," Captain Sanchez Zamora reveals.

"L- l- like what?" Lieutenant Ortega Revelo asks.

"I don't deal with the past very much, Lieutenant," Captain Sanchez Zamora says.

Lieutenant Ortega Revelo nods and says: "So he w- w- w-as one of us."

Captain Sanchez Zamora tenses up for a split second. But it's a split second only.

"The slanderer kills a thousand times; the assassin but once. No, he wasn't one of us. I don't think that people want to be like us," he admits. "What do the other witnesses say?"

"Right," Lieutenant Ortega Revelo continues to look at his notes while Captain Sanchez Zamora devours the wedding cake. "Alejandro Mateo Torres Estrada... Hold on. Wa- wa- wa-sn't he the guy from Radio Tro- Tro- Tro-picana? The guy with the coiffure? Always in the pa- pa- pa-pers? My fiancee, she loved that g- g- guy. And his h- h- h-air. Wow! Anyway, Alejandro Mateo Torres Estrada left the party with an unknown wo- wo-wo-man. At around eight."

"Says who?" Captain Sanchez Zamora asks as Lieutenant Ortega Revelo points at Alejandro Mateo Torres Estrada's best man who sits on a bench smoking a cigarette looking all ravaged.

Captain Sanchez Zamora chews and nods.

"Five f- f- f-oot something, eighty pounds. Maybe less. Red dr- dr- dr-ess. Angelic. Arrived on a m- m- m-otorcycle," Lieutenant Ortega Revelo says.

"It was someone who was supposed to be a friend but obviously didn't see it that way," Captain Sanchez Zamora declares.

"She c- c- c-ould've pushed him. Self-defence is always an o- o- o-ption," Lieutenant Ortega Revelo guesses.

¡El idiota!

"How many angels dance on the head of a pin?" Captain Sanchez Zamora asks.

Lieutenant Ortega Revelo briefly tries to figure it out.

¡El estúpido!

"Maybe he was m- m- m-ixed up in organized crime. After all, he was in sh- sh- sh-ow business," he says as Captain Sanchez Zamora lifts his MD eyebrow again.

"Organized crime controls violence and distributes it properly," he says. "No. The victim didn't have the stomach for it. Never had. I just want you to think big, Lieutenant, for Christ sakes! Look, a simple rule in dealing with those who are hard to get along with is to remember that this person is striving to assert his superiority; and you must deal with him from that point of view."

"Maybe he just had a g- g- g-ood time, kinda, warmed himself up for the b- b- b-ig night, felt guilty and j- j- j-umped," Lieutenant Ortega Revelo guesses.

Captain Sanchez Zamora looks fed up.

"Lieutenant, find me that woman," he orders.

"You th- th- th-ink...," Lieutenant Ortega Revelo begins.

"I think that everything has to do with everything," Captain Sanchez Zamora says.

"Yes, *patron*," Lieutenant Ortega Revelo says as he's about to leave but then has a final thought.

"I still don't u- u- u-nderstand," he says, "why are the best chefs in the world m- m- m-en?"

Captain Sanchez Zamora grinds his jaws.

¡El imbécil!

"I mean," Lieutenant Ortega Revelo continues, "m- m- m-en expect to get p- p- p-aid for their work, right? Women do most of the free coo- coo- coo-king. It's like a pa- pa- pa-ssion, no?"

"Lieutenant," Captain Sanchez Zamora says.

"Yes, *p- p- p-atron*," Lieutenant Ortega Revelo answers.

"If you were a shoemaker people would be born without feet," Captain Sanchez Zamora announces.

"Yes, *p- p- p-atron*," Lieutenant Ortega Revelo agrees as he's about to light a cigarette.

"For the sake of your family," Captain Sanchez Zamora blasts, "for the sake of your family, your friends and your career, please end your suicidal path."

Lieutenant Ortega Revelo looks at the cigarette and decides against smoking it. Captain Sanchez Zamora nods fatherly, smiles at him and says: "No matter if the child's born with a flat nose, as long as it breathes."

¡El fracasado!

As Lieutenant Ortega Revelo leaves, Captain Sanchez Zamora stares into the cloudy sky, scratching his beefy neck.

"The sky looks beautiful, and I'm honored to be at work tonight," he says. "We should consider every day lost on which we have not danced at least once. And we should call every truth false which was not accompanied by at least one laugh. Without music, life would be a mistake."

Captain Sanchez Zamora finishes the wedding cake with one last bite as he begins to tap dance while humming his favorite tune: *Adoracion.*

Monday morning, April 11, 2016. Back in Las Peñas. At the foot of Santa Ana Hill Chapel. A short, dead-end road. Numa Pompilio Lana. Paved with uneven, century-old cobblestones. Colourful wooden houses. Many beautifully restored. But part of the area's charm derives from the flaking paint and gentle disrepair of those who haven't. A couple of cannons point towards the Guayas River honouring the city's stalwart resistance to seventeenth-century pirates. What used to be a slum, today shines as Guayaquil's prettiest corner.

Dressed like an inconspicuous Ecuadorian girl, T-Shirt, Jeans and Flip-Flops, our heroine approaches a public telephone.

She picks up the receiver, throws some coins in the machine and dials a number.

She waits.

She looks to the right.

She looks to the left.

Someone picks up at the other end of the line. Our heroine responds. And listens.

She appears to be frazzled.

Once more she looks over her shoulders. Suddenly her expressions and demeanor change.

Her face radiates.

She's all over the moon.

She speaks into the phone. And listens again.

Then she hangs up as big tears roll down her face.

Quickly she disappears into a crowd of local pedestrians and tourists.

Our heroine.

The girl with the magnificent body and enticing personality. *¡Niña!*

Friday afternoon, April 15, 2016. Urdesa. Once an upper class neighborhood with mansions and beautiful gardens, today all villas got a garden fence for security reasons. The rich have moved to Los Ceibos or Samborondón. Only those who do not want to accept the present, are still there.

Our heroine's dressed like a frumpy *Hausfrau.* She waits in front of a what once must have been a lavish home. A pitted scarf covers her hair. The housekeeper, a chubby lady in her late sixties, exits through the gate.

"I'm sorry," our heroine asks, "does *Señor* Santos Calderon still live here?"

The housekeeper eyes her suspiciously.

"Who wants to know?" she asks.

"*Señor* Santos Calderon and I are old acquaintances," our heroine answers.

¡Cierra el pico!

The housekeeper laughs.

"You don't say," she says.

Our heroine looks to the ground and begins to snivel. She's making a helluva show of holding back a flood of tears.

"I'm in a very delicate situation," she says as the housekeeper quickly begins to feel sorry for her.

"What's the matter, my dear?" she says.

Our heroine, not wanting to lose her point, looks up to the housekeeper.

"I've nowhere to go. I need help," our heroine pleads.

"My poor thing," the housekeeper says, "why don't you see *Señor* Santos Calderon at his office?"

"I'm only a helpless *niña*," our heroine replies as she hands an envelope to the housekeeper who hesitates to accept it.

"Please!" our heroine begs.

The housekeeper thinks for a few seconds - and takes the letter. For the first time she unbends to the extent of giving forth a scrupulous smile.

"Today's his birthday. Today might be your lucky day," the housekeeper says.

Our heroine smiles back.

Big time!

"Say," she says, "is *Señora* Santos Calderon in?"

"There's never been a *Señora* Santos Calderon. Unless you mean *Señor* Santos Calderon's mother. But she's passed on."

"Thank you," our heroine sighs as she relaxes and exchanges a relieved and triumphant glance with the housekeeper.

¡La picara!

The motive always defines the appearance.

While kissing the housekeeper's hands, our heroine says: "Stronger than a mother's love."

Speaking of the devil's mother...

Señor Ricardo Miguel Santos Calderon has a face only a mother can love. In his late forties as well, he's a preening nostril flarer.

¡El guache!

Just wait and see.

While our heroine's talking to his housekeeper, *Señor* Ricardo Miguel Santos Calderon sits behind his office desk. His secretary stands by the door. She trembles.

Just for the record: this guy runs one of the biggest export and import businesses in the country. His company is located in the port of Guayaquil. Needless to footnote that *Señor* Ricardo Miguel Santos Calderon is one of the richest men in all of South America. But as the old whore says: nobody on this continent got rich on his own. *Señor* Ricardo Miguel Santos made sure that his place did not burn down like many others. He got everything covered. God bless, but *Señor* Ricardo Miguel Santos Calderon plugged into a power grid the rest of the people built for him. That's his legacy. And that he too went to the CAH.

¡El capullo!

¡Este es Guayaquil!

"The funeral's tomorrow," *Señor* Ricardo Miguel Santos Calderon's secretary utters.

"Why?" he screams with an expression of mingled amazement and rage.

He yanks a sheet of paper out of a vintage typewriter. (*Señor* Ricardo Miguel Santos Calderon does not believe in modern technology.) A look of infinite weariness and disgust covers his face.

"They said," his secretary begins, "they said they wouldn't bury him on a Sunday. They're too busy. I'm so sorry."

Señor Ricardo Miguel Santos Calderon begins to put on a show of bitter reproach as he leans back in his swivel chair.

"Me too," he says. "We work on Saturdays. What did your husband die of?"

"A long illness," his secretary replies.

"A long illness," *Señor* Ricardo Miguel Santos Calderon repeats.

"A very long illness," his secretary says.

Señor Ricardo Miguel Santos Calderon's voice is matter of fact, almost casual.

"Indeed," he says, "It is what it is. Every donkey has its own saddle. Let bygones be bygones, shall we? After all, today's my birthday."

"Thank you, *Señor*, thank you so much," *Señor* Ricardo Miguel Santos Calderon's secretary says while she approaches the desk reaching out her hand.

Señor Ricardo Miguel Santos Calderon looks scarred.

"To learn the human mind, wander with human heart through the world. Hands that give also receive," she says.

Señor Ricardo Miguel Santos Calderon reluctantly shakes her hand.

"You're a good man, *Señor*. Thank you," the secretary says and scrams out of the office.

Señor Ricardo Miguel Santos Calderon cleans his hands with a wet wipe and picks up the phone.

"Human resources?", he asks and continues, "look, my girl, her name's... Exactly. That's the one. I've an issue. She's tardy. At times she doesn't show up at all. Repeatedly. And tomorrow..."

Señor Ricardo Miguel Santos Calderon pauses and listens.

"What work council?" he asks and...

¡El pajero!

"That's why this country's *kaput*," he screams and throws the phone back on the cradle.

It bounces off, and he has to hang up again. This time *Señor* Ricardo Miguel Santos Calderon slams it down.

"Quite simply, this country's lost its way," he says to himself full of anger...

...which still lingers in his mood as he arrives home in Urdesa a few hours later driving his beloved black Audi Q7 SUV.

In front of his gate lies an empty can of coke. Señor Ricardo Miguel Santos Calderon stops the vehicle and exits. He picks up the canister and spies to all sides.

Señor Ricardo Miguel Santos Calderon tries to uncover the polluter. But nobody's in sight. Irritated he climbs back into the car. The gate opens. *Señor* Ricardo Miguel Santos Calderon drives on his property and enters his house where he throws the can into the trash bin as he looks at the kitchen table.

A half-chicken dinner waits on a plate and looks as foul as his mood. It's covered with plastic wrap. *Señor* Ricardo Miguel Santos Calderon sighs as he discovers our heroine's letter which rests behind the plate.

He picks up the letter, sniffs it out, regards it a moment, moistens a finger and opens it. *Señor* Ricardo Miguel Santos Calderon reads the message carefully and grins. At once he describes the food.

"He who does not go to sea knows not how to pray," he says and leaves the kitchen...

...and arrives only a few minutes later at the Riviera Restaurant at Victor Emilio Estrada 707 not too far from his home.

The Riviera is a richly appointed eatery, awe-inspiring in its dignified furnishings which shriek of class.

The food is Italian.

A hostess waits expectantly.

Señor Ricardo Miguel Santos Calderon stalks in bravely and before he can utter a word, the hostess escorts him inside the place in which quite a number of people are seated at their tables.

Señor Ricardo Miguel Santos Calderon regards them with a curious expression as he approaches our heroine who still wonders if the future has a cure for the past, who sits at a table for two and who looks into a hand mirror surveying herself with straightforward approval.

She's dressed in an almost transparent silk organza garment. Her hair's long and curly. She looks stunning.

As *Señor* Ricardo Miguel Santos Calderon and the hostess arrive, our heroine pulls out a curl of hair before each ear. The hostess hospitably indicates the table to *Señor* Santos Calderon.

"It's a magical night. Please enjoy," she says and leaves.

Our heroine puts the hand mirror back into her large handbag. Incredulously *Señor* Ricardo Miguel Santos Calderon stares at her.

"Sit down, Ricardo Miguel," our heroine demands.

¡Me importa una mierda!

Señor Ricardo Miguel Santos Calderon remains standing and watches her with a peculiar expression.

"Who are you?" he asks.

"Gentleness is stronger than severity, water is stronger than rock, love is stronger than force. I'm the fearful mermaid who serves her winded lovers' bones in brine," our heroine says with a twinkle in her eyes.

Señor Ricardo Miguel Santos Calderon smiles at this unexpected statement, sits down and eyeballs at our heroine critically.

"She was lying," our heroine says.

Señor Ricardo Miguel Santos Calderon reacts disturbed.

"She said you were handsome," our heroine continues.

Señor Ricardo Miguel Santos Calderon reacts disappointed now.

"You're dashing, Ricardo Miguel," our heroine says with a big smile as *Señor* Ricardo Miguel Santos Calderon smirks happily and pinches his nose.

There's the sound of a piano chord being struck. Again, it's *Adoracion.* The waitress arrives with the wine card.

"Today's special is the *Risotto con Camarones...*," she begins as *Señor* Ricardo Miguel Santos Calderon, without looking at the waitress, dismisses her with a wave of his hand.

"*No te preocupes. Yo invito,*" our heroine says.

"I don't drink," he answers.

Our heroine never takes her eyes off him and ignores his rudeness.

She studies him.

He studies her.

The waitress leaves.

"You're a Christian, Ricardo Miguel?" our heroine asks.

"Faith is a force. A powerful force," he answers. "It's seen me through the good times. But also through some personal tragedies."

"Your mother," our heroine says.

"My mother, yes," *Señor* Ricardo Miguel Santos Calderon says. "God bless her heart."

Tenderly our heroine puts her hand on his and says: "There can be no true pleasantry without discretion."

"I did not know how to make my own bed. My mother took care of that," *Señor* Ricardo Miguel Santos Calderon answers.

Our heroine pretends that she's genuinely interested in him and his grief.

"Of course, she did," she says.

"She wanted me to be on top of the world. She always listened to me," he answers.

"A quality most women don't have," our heroine says.

"People never understood us," he answers.

"People believe the worst," she says.

"People are as cold as charity," he answers. "They frighten me."

Suddenly *Señor* Ricardo Miguel Santos Calderon looks very glum and depressed.

"I'm afraid, too," our heroine says, "and therefore unquestioningly obedient. Happy birthday, Ricardo Miguel. This one's for you!"

Our heroine leans over and kisses him passionately. *Señor* Santos Calderon's face breaks into a happy grin. Our heroine's got him by the balls.

"*Me gustas mucho.* Let's go home," she proposes.

Señor Ricardo Miguel Santos Calderon assumes a conciliatory attitude.

"Yeah," he agrees, "but let me go pupu first."

Señor Ricardo Miguel Santos Calderon gets up and leaves for the men's room. Our heroine turns an acid smile on the approaching waitress.

¡El cochino!

Only thirty minutes later...

...she's in *Señor* Ricardo Miguel Santos Calderon's villa. The lights are off.

"It was my girl, wasn't it," he says.

"I didn't know you had a girl," our heroine answers.

"I'm talking about my secretary," he says. "She arranged everything, didn't she? What would I do without her? Such a good *niña.*"

¡Niña!

"Where are you taking me, Ricardo Miguel?" our heroine asks.

"Let's try to make the best use of my limited abilities," *Señor* Ricardo Miguel Santos Calderon answers.

He turns on the lights. They've arrived in his bedroom. It's very plush and pink with a huge portrait of *Señor* Ricardo Miguel Santos Calderon and his mother on the wall. He approaches our heroine and grabs her by the waist.

"Ricardo Miguel," she says with mock perplexity, "a good girl must always keep her skirt down."

¡Hostia puta!

Suddenly our heroine realizes that there's something sinister about *Señor* Ricardo Miguel Santos Calderon.

She takes a step back and looks him over carefully as she begins to realize that all is not well as it could be. Her body stiffens.

"Little by little one walks far," she says as *Señor* Ricardo Miguel Santos Calderon flares in anger. His tone is unmistakable now.

"Who says I wanna good girl?" he says. "Show 'em to me!"

Señor Ricardo Miguel Santos Calderon approaches our heroine anew.

"Show you what, Ricardo Miguel?" she says. "Think of your mother."

Señor Ricardo Miguel Santos Calderon grabs our heroine who drops her handbag.

"My mother was a bitch in heat. Schlampe. Hure. Fuck my mother! Fuck you! *Schlampen. Schlampen. Huren. Alles Huren.* You're all part of a demonic conspiracy!" he shouts at the top of his lungs mixing Spanish with German as he pushes our heroine against the wall reaching between her legs and...

"What's this?" he asks.

...rips the Bond Arms Cowboy Defender Derringer Pistol from her thigh holder. He squeezes it against our heroine's head.

"Ricardo Miguel, I don't want to court any harm. I'm a good girl," our heroine says.

¡Mierda!

"You lying cunt," he answers, "you won't listen, will you?"

Señor Ricardo Miguel Santos Calderon hits our heroine with the firearm. He then throws her on the floor and points the gun at her as he crosses to a chaise longue and sits down. Our heroine's eyes fill with fear. She has an open wound. Her temple's bleeding.

Señor Ricardo Miguel Santos Calderon gives her a gesture as if to say 'get to work.' Our heroine knows what he demands. She crawls to him and ends up between his legs. She looks daggers at him and undoes his trousers.

Our heroine takes his cock out and moves her head forward. *Señor* Ricardo Miguel Santos Calderon stops her though.

He takes her hand and grasps it around his penis keeping his own hand over the top. Like this, he masturbates as quick and hard as humanly possible until he swiftly comes with some genuine pain. *Señor* Ricardo Miguel Santos Calderon releases our heroine's hand and begins to suck his thump.

"Oh, mother," *Señor* Ricardo Miguel Santos Calderon mumbles.

Our heroine still glares at him.

"May I go to the bathroom, *Señor*?" she asks kindly.

Señor Ricardo Miguel Santos Calderon leans further back and grunts.

Our heroine gets up. She turns around, goes to her handbag, picks it up, opens it and takes something out. She then makes a complete turn and faces *Señor* Ricardo Miguel Santos Calderon again holding a syringe in her hand.

"How's this?" she asks.

¡Concho!

Señor Ricardo Miguel Santos Calderon's totally stupefied. He has no time to react as our heroine leaps on him in full fury.

Señor Ricardo Miguel Santos Calderon drops the gun. It plummets between the cushions. Our heroine jams the needle in his neck and empties the ampoule into his cervical artery.

"I bring a message from Jorge Adalberto Icaza Ortiz," she says. "You've thirty seconds to respond."

Señor Ricardo Miguel Santos Calderon's eyes express terror and mortification. Like before him Erick Andres Pena Segale's aka Antonio de la Cruz's and Alejandro Mateo Torres Estrada's eyes too.

"Redeem yourself, Ricardo Miguel Santos Calderon," our heroine offers graciously.

But *Señor* Ricardo Miguel Santos Calderon doesn't give a fuck about atonement. He spits in our heroine's face. She doesn't react. His saliva glissades down her features as *Señor* Ricardo Miguel Santos Calderon passes out and our heroine gets up. She grabs her handbag and strides into the adjoining bathroom.

Our heroine looks at herself in the mirror.

She takes her wig off and drops it on the sink.

She turns on the water.

She inspects her bleeding wound and cleans it.

She takes off her attire.

She puts cold water in the tub for a bath.

She takes her handbag and leaves the bathroom.

Señor Ricardo Miguel Santos Calderon still sits slumped on the chaise longue.

Our heroine opens her handbag.

Everything the needs she finds therein.

Everything she's about to do she does with precision.

Our heroine begins by putting a plastic sheet on the bed.

She hoists the unconscious *Señor* Ricardo Miguel Santos Calderon on top of it, legs facing the headboard to make the next step easier.

She places a rolled towel under his neck positioning him as if he were about to get mouth-to-mouth resuscitation.

She slowly pushes a long, well-oiled rubber tube down his throat, carefully so as not to choke him. She then attaches a small funnel to the top of the pipe.

She starts to drop a variety of pills into the tube adding water to ensure the pills reach *Señor* Ricardo Miguel Santos Calderon's stomach.

She pulls down his unzipped corduroys and underwear.

She holds up his legs.

She inserts a suppository of concentrated sedatives and a fever-causing agent into his rectum.

She pulls up his slip and breeches again, leaves for bathroom, turns off the water and returns to *Señor* Ricardo Miguel Santos Calderon.

She puts a thermometer band on his forehead.

She observes his temperature.

She looks at her wristwatch. It's 9.15 P.M.

She looks at the thermometer band.

Señor Ricardo Miguel Santos Calderon has developed a high fever. He's broiling.

Our heroine gets up and walks to the kitchen where she eyes *Señor* Ricardo Miguel Santos Calderon's half-chicken dinner on the table.

She rips the plastic wrap off the plate and tears a leg out of the roasted animal.

She stuffs it in her mouth.

She opens the freezer and takes two large plastic bags of ice cubes out.

She empties the bags into the bathtub.

The half-eaten chicken leg's still in her mouth as she pulls *Señor* Ricardo Miguel Santos Calderon from the bedroom into the bathroom.

With her last strength our heroine puts him in the bathtub. The shock of the glacial water causes his body to jolt.

"Wicked," our heroine whispers as the abrupt change in temperature with the influence of the medication brings what looks like a heart attack to *Señor* Ricardo Miguel Santos Calderon.

¡Hijo de puta!

Without warning *Señor* Ricardo Miguel Santos Calderon regains consciousness.

Our heroine jumps back.

He stares at her.

His eyes are wide open.

He can hardly breathe.

His voice sounds guttural.

"*Coño.* You got me. But you won't get everybody," he says foaming at the mouth.

While eating the rest of the chicken leg our heroine observes as *Señor* Ricardo Miguel Santos Calderon slowly ceases to exist until...

...he suddenly jumps up one more time.

"Top of the world, Ma. I'm coming home," he shrieks with his last breath while sliding back into the ice-cold bath his face frozen in consternation...

...as it is an hour later when Captain Sanchez Zamora and Lieutenant Ortega Revelo look at it.

"There was no cloud above his head. Not even a mist," Captain Sanchez Zamora says. "All the merchandise that got in and out of Ecuador did not pass through the Gulf of Guayaquil, Lieutenant, it passed through his hands. Without Ricardo the Malecón 2000 would still be the same rotten waterfront promenade it's always been. He invented the Nuevo Parque Histórico. Put seven million dollars of his own money in it. We owe..."

"In what ca- ca- ca-pacity were you and *Señor* Santos Calderon friendly, *pa- pa- pa-tron*?" Lieutenant Ortega Revelo interrupts him as Captain Sanchez Zamora's lost in speculation as to how to proceed.

He beholds the dead man in the bathtub.

"*Señor* Santos Calderon didn't have any friends at school, didn't want any. He felt better being alone. He sat on a bench and watched the others play and they looked foolish to him. Still, he invested loads of money in the CAH. Loved it there. Loved their teachers. Loved us. Loved his mother. *Wir liebten dich*," Captain Sanchez Zamora says. "A prime soul checked out tonight."
Lieutenant Ortega Revelo looks around with a scowl.

"E- e- e-nemies?" he asks.

"Enemies?" Captain Sanchez Zamora asks. "A man with no enemies is what, Lieutenant? A man with no character. Only people can make one another suffer so. But always forgive your enemies. Nothing annoys them so much."

Captain Sanchez Zamora removes his glasses, dries his teary eyes and blows his nose.

"C'mon," Lieutenant Ortega Revelo says. "You must've been a t- t- t-ough kid."

¡Vaca ignorante!

"I was afraid my eyes would get knocked out if there was too much of a rough and tumble play," Captain Sanchez Samora answers. "The other boys called me four eyes. I couldn't look a girl in the eye. Or a boy... To tell the truth, Lieutenant, I was kind of a sissy. That sounds rather feminine, doesn't it? Mamma says I was intended for a girl anyway. It made me pretty mad to be told so, but I guess it was partly so. *Señor* Santos Calderon understood. Yes, we were friendly. In many capacities, Lieutenant. I'm telling you, you only live once, but if you do it right, once is enough."

Captain Sanchez Zamora looks at Lieutenant Ortega Revelo who offers him a Nicorette stop smoking gum.

"I'm l- l- l-earnin'. I'm learnin'," Lieutenant Ortega Revolo says.

"Be yourself, Gino. Everyone else is already taken," Captain Sanchez Zamora says with a smile.

He exits the bathroom. Lieutenant Ortega Revelo follows him into the bedroom while stuffing a piece of gum into this mouth. He trips and almost falls flat on his face as the other cops are sweeping the crime scene.

A policeman is taking photographs.

A second officer is collecting fingerprints.

And so on.

Majestically Captain Sanchez Zamora strides through the bedroom which shows no mark whatsoever of what has actually happened. Our heroine did an (almost) perfect job leaving no traces.

"With the benefit of hindsight I wish I had done more," Captain Sanchez Zamora says as a policewoman approaches him.

She hands him our heroine's pistol that *Señor* Ricardo Miguel Santos Calderon had dropped.

"Found it on the sofa," she says.

"Found it on the sofa?" Captain Sanchez Zamora repeats.

"Yes, Captain," she says as Captain Sanchez Zamora points at the chaise longue giving her the MD eyebrow.

"This, Sergeant, is called what?" he asks the policewoman. "I know, I can be a nitpicker about details that seem to be over the top but then again I'm into what I'm into so a lot of people forgive me because of it. Paying attention pays these days, *niña*."

Captain Sanchez Zamora accepts the gun and hands it over to Lieutenant Ortega Revelo as the policewoman reacts annoyed to Captain Sanchez Zamora's belittlement.

"Captain", she hisses.

"Captain?" Captain Sanchez Zamora repeats. "Try Major."

"Yes, Major," she says.

"I almost forgot, *pa- pa- pa-tron*," Lieutenant Ortega Revelo says. "Congratulations, M- m- m-ajor."

Sanchez Zamora couldn't care less about Lieutenant Ortega Revelo's conduct. Captain. Major. He's just doing his job and is happy to do so. Major Sanchez Zamora doesn't need promotions. His ego is intact. He looks at the gun.

"Lovely choice," he says.

"You think it be- be- be-longs...," Lieutenant Ortega Revelo begins.

"I think it fits comfortably in a pocket holster. Or in a purse," Major Sanchez Zamora says.

"Give it to the lab boys. But do it personally."

Lieutenant Ortega Revelo takes the gun.

"W- w- w-ait a second," he says, "remember the taxi driver? He was shot with a small ca- ca- ca-liber gun."

"Antonio was a solid driver," Major Sanchez Zamora says.

"You're ki- ki- ki-lling me, patron," Lieutenant Ortega Revelo says. "Who in this town don't you know? Antonio de la Cr- cr- cr-uz was a common cr- cr- cr-iminal. He went by several identities. There was a wa- wa-wa-rrant out for his arrest."

Before Major Sanchez Zamora has a chance to respond, they're approached by another cop.

"Nothing", he says, "dude took a bath. Dude had a heart attack. Dude's dead."

"The du- du- du-de was dre- dre- dre-ssed," Lieutenant Ortega Revelo says anxiously.

"Who's this *mocoso*?" the cop says to Major Sanchez Zamora while looking at Lieutenant Ortega Revelo. "Look, young man, this is Guayakills. You'll see more *mierda* in your life."

The cop leaves as Major Sanchez Zamora walks to the window and looks outside.

It's a hot night.

Once again.

But no stars.

Once again.

No moon.

As always.

Just another fucking hot night in fucking...

¡Este es Guayakills!

"Look at that. That's the thing! Cause the whole country is like this - more so - even. And that's why I never have a doubt that this nation will be a great nation soon. I hope that some of my dissents will one day be the law," Major Sanchez Zamora says. "Anyway, the world is so empty if one thinks only of mountains, rivers and cities, but to know someone who thinks and feels with us, who, though distant, is close to us in spirit, this makes the earth for us an inhabitant garden."

During his last remarks *Señor* Santos Calderon's housekeeper sweeps in.

"In this world, everything's up to God," she says. "You wanted to see me?"

The housekeeper troops directly to the bathroom and peeks inside.

"He's dead, right?" she says to Lieutenant Ortega Revelo. "Am I right?"

Before Lieutenant Ortega Revelo has a chance to respond, the housekeeper seats herself on the chaise longue never letting the bathroom door out of her sight.

"*Señor* Santos Calderon was the devil," she says.

"*Señor* Santos Calderon was the devil?" Major Sanchez Zamora repeats as he approaches the house-keeper.

"The devil's wiser more on account of his age than on account of being the devil. You believe in the devil, Officer?" she continues.

¡La picara!

The housekeeper's not intimidated by Major Sanchez Zamora. She looks straight into his eyes.

"Yes," he answers her question. "But not too much."

"God never says but," the housekeeper says as Major Sanchez Zamora seats himself beside her on the chaise longue.

"I'd rather serve the devil I know than the devil I don't know," the housekeeper says. "Sure hope that pretty thing..."

"Pretty th- th- th-ing?" Lieutenant Ortega Revelo straightaway absorbed by her last remark interrupts her. "What pretty th- th- th-ing?"

The housekeeper is in awe and wonder now.

"She had the creamiest and loveliest skin one is likely to see. Like a Hershey's chocolate bar. A face ripe for dreaming about," the housekeeper says.

"We're loo- loo- loo-king for a girl with a fair body and a sick mi- mi- mi-nd," Lieutenant Ortega Revelo says as Major Sanchez Zamora dismisses his effort to be rough with the housekeeper and puts his arm around her shoulder.

"I'm selfish, impatient and a little insecure," he says. "I make mistakes, I am out of control and at times hard to handle. But if you can't handle me at my worst, then you sure as hell don't deserve me at my best. But I'm a mild man too, a tolerant man with great capacity to understand others. You came back tonight. Late? Around 10 P.M. Why?"

The housekeeper breathes out and puts her cheek against Major Sanchez Zamora's arm.

"I'm a pleasant person with good teeth," she says. "Unlike my mother, I don't have a naturally smiley face. But the quickest way to a man's heart is through his stomach. I felt sorry for *Señor* Santos Calderon. After all, it was his birthday. I baked him a birthday cake. A gluten-free sunken apple cake with whipped cream. I call it my Wednesday cake because it can easily be made during the week when time is short. On Fridays too. You don't happen to like cakes, Officer, do you? I use a secret ingredient."

Major Sanchez Zamora gives her his brightest grin.

"I love secrets. Did you say gluten-free?" he asks.

The housekeeper smiles happily back.

"Don't go anywhere," she whispers. "I use double cream."

"Cross my heart and hope to die," Major Sanchez Zamora gesticulates as the housekeeper rises and leaves.

Lieutenant Ortega Revelo gets all stirred up.

"She kn- kn- kn-ows her," he screams. "We go- go- go-t her! Hey, pretty *ni- ni- ni-ña*, time to wake u- u- u-p!"

Major Sanchez Zamora returns to the window. He laughs loud and raucously.

"Not yet, Lieutenant, not yet," he says. "But she's living on what?"

Lieutenant Ortega Revelo throws him a puzzled look.

"A wise girl kisses, but doesn't love, listens but doesn't believe, and leaves before she's left. She's living on velvet," Major Sanchez Zamora says and repeats, "she's living on velvet."

Major Sanchez Zamora begins to whistle.

Adoracion.

What else?

And begins to tap dance.

Just a little...

At about the same time in Las Peñas. A Zen style studio apartment. The room is filled with steam. Only outlines and forms are visible. The steam effuses from under the bathroom door. Everything is fogged up and opaque. Our heroine's seated in a small bathtub. Hunched over, her breathing speeds up. But it also becomes erratic. Eventually our heroine starts striking the water. With both fists. With all her might. She begins to scream. With stamina. With forte. And a monumental as well as touching crescendo...

¡El bastardo!

Saturday morning, April 16, 2016. Our heroine watches as rabbi Nepomuk Glass leaves the Santa Ana Hill Chapel. He looks haggard. His eyes are empty, glazed over.

Our heroine approaches Nepomuk whose countenance resembles someone leaving the courtroom in defeat.

Nepomuk, startled by the noise of our heroine's high heels, looks up. He turns around and smiles at our heroine in a heartbeat. Nepomuk's face brightens as he notices our heroine's beaten face but doesn't say anything. He's a gentleman.

Our heroine's dressed in a simple blue garment. For the first time she looks attractive without trying. Despite her bruised temple and black eye.

"Saturday morning, isn't it?" she says as she continues to walk towards Nepomuk.

"Yes," he answers. "But you missed my service. Actually, everybody missed my service."

"I'm sorry," our heroine answers.

"If I'm not for myself, who will be there for me? But if I'm for myself alone, what am I? And if not now, when?" he says. "Here we are again. If you find a *Mensch,* you're in good hands. You hungry?"

Our heroine considers.

"Famished," she says.

Nepomuk hands her his knapsack and takes our heroine's arm.

"Sometimes you climb out of bed in the morning and you think, I'm not gonna make it, but you laugh inside, remembering all the times you've felt that way. C'mon," Nepomuk says as he begins to walk down the 444 steps to the foot of the hill where he lives nearby in a modest house.

Our heroine looks at a print of Van Gogh's painting *Shoes* which hangs on a wall. She then strides through Nepomuk's living room that is filled with books, papers and international magazines. Der Spiegel. Die Zeit. Die Frankfurter Allgemeine Zeitung. The Economist. There's a small television set, a recliner chair, and an antique gramophone as well as plenty of records. Candles are lit. The place is very *gemütlich*. Cozy. A photograph shows Nepomuk as a younger man with his daughter who's wearing a white ballet dress.

While our heroine's inspecting Nepomuk's home, he's in the kitchen stirring the soup that's on the stove. His sleeves are rolled up. On his left forearm there's a tattooed number: 202499.

"Home is where the books are. All is foreseen, yet free-will is given to man," he says loud enough so our heroine can hear him. "Wonder if my daughter will come with her kids. She's a ballet teacher. David might be working though. They respect each other's space. What does that mean? It means nothing. They're just avoiding each other's flaws. As if those matters. When marrying, ask yourself the question: do you believe that you will be able to converse well with this person into old age? Everything else in marriage is transitory. Try to learn to breathe deeply, to really taste food when you eat, and when you sleep, to really sleep. Try as much as possible to be wholly alive with all your might, and when you laugh, laugh like hell. And when you get angry, get good and angry. Try to be alive. You will be dead soon enough."

Nepomuk lights a cigarette as our heroine glances into the interconnecting shteibl, Nepomuk's miniature synagogue.

"Molding us to perfection only leads to madness," he continues. "The world's not ideal, you know. It's not absolute. Maybe that's why I feel happy on this planet. I divide it into two halves though. Those places where I cannot stay and those to which I can't go. So, I better make the best of it. Darkness cannot drive out darkness. Only light can do that. Hate cannot drive out hate. Only love can do that. A day without sunshine is like, you know, night."

Our heroine lights up too now and joins Nepomuk in his kitchen. He says: "I don't know why I should especially associate myself with any particular country just because of where I was born. Maybe it shaped my personality. Who knows? Potentially every country is all countries. My daughter always asks, what does all this mean to you? What a question is that? What am I supposed to answer? Anyway, we're all dying, aren't we? All the husbands and all the wives, and not teaching each other what we really know. The minute you start fiddling around outside the idea of monogamy, nothing satisfies you anymore."

Our heroine listens attentively as Nepomuk tastes the soup, adds salt and pepper and stirs it anew. He says: "My daughter and David, they're all about diversity. Seeking the truth anywhere but in themselves. A new fetish every year. Recycling. Organic food. Animal rights.

Global warming. I think they don't see the forest before the trees. And then the two boys. They're *schlepping* them from this to that and back. Prep-shul for anxiety, if you ask me. What's the void they're trying to fill? Life's a narrow bridge. I've done the most awful rubbish in order to have somewhere to go in the morning. You never mentioned your name."

Our heroine leaves the kitchen and skims through an ancient copy of Rainer Maria Rilke's *Book of Hours*. The volume is full of scribbles.

"Right," Nepomuk responds and after a brief moment of silence says: "Acknowledge your fears. Find a place inside where there's joy, and the joy will burn out the pain. Knowing your own darkness is the best method for dealing with the darkness of other people. Seek conviction. As they say in A.A., there're two reasons to go to the meetings. Because you want to. And because you don't want to. So, you keep on going. It works. Well, I'm doing my part as a good citizen. Always have. Though at times I've been misunderstood. We've been misunderstood. Many a man fails as an original thinker simply because his memory is too good. A subject for a great book would be God's boredom after the seventh day of creation. Well, there's no greater agony than bearing an untold story inside you."

Nepomuk walks into the living room with two soup plates. He moves more easily now. Nepomuk smiles at our heroine.

"I welcome the angel into my house," he says.

Our heroine smiles at him and puts the book back on the shelf.

"Let's eat while it's hot," Nepomuk says as he sets the table with the plates of black-eyed pea soup. Our heroine and Nepomuk sit down. They're drinking water and begin to eat.

"Where's your wife?" our heroine asks after a while.

"Oh, she's gone," Nepomuk answers.

"I'm sorry," our heroine responds.

Nepomuk laughs. Our heroine smiles sheepishly.

"No. Not gone-gone," he says. "She didn't like it here. Thought the city was lost, decaying. That time was running out. Well, Guayaquil has been good to me, but that wasn't a gift. And I was up to, I'm told by my daughter, of course, you don't remember if you drink that much, about two-and-a-half to three bottles of hard liquor a day. It's rather nice to have gone through it, to have survived this one too. Regret is useless in life. It's in the past. All we have is now. I still smoke too much. I think it gives my voice an edge."

"Everybody deserves a second chance," our heroine says. "Everybody."

Nepomuk smiles at our heroine like a father at his daughter.

"I'm almost healthy enough for a new wife. I'm not sure if I'm attractive enough though. I used to be handsome as a Prussian prince," Nepomuk says. "How's the soup?"

"Very good, thank you," our heroine answers.

Nepomuk looks happy.

"Tell me," he asks, "why did you come here? Why did you come to this town?"

Our heroine weighs her words before speaking.

"I came here to make the impact as I see fit to do so," she says.

Nepomuk nods as our heroine looks at him as if she was waiting for yet another question.

"You meet your destiny on the road you take to avoid it," he says. "I learned a long time ago not to disagree on things that I don't have a solid opinion about, and I don't believe too much in advice. I never got any, so I don't give any, and for those who believe in God, most of the big questions are answered. I'm braced for disappointment though. That's part of life too."

"You believe in life after death?" our heroine asks.

"What matters most is how well you walk through fire, no? Until your faith returns," Nepomuk says. "The cave you fear to enter holds the treasure you seek. And the cure must be as convincing as the illness."

Our heroine stops eating.

"You believe God will forgive us for what we've done?" she asks.

Nepomuk stops eating too. He places the spoon next to his plate.

"Wrong question," he says. "Will God forgive us for what we didn't do?"

Our heroine nods.

"I was a sinner. I slugged some people. I hurt many people. And it's true, I never looked back to see the casualties," Nepomuk continues. "Guilt dwells in every chest. Sometimes it's good to be hated. What do you regard as most humane? To spare someone shame? More soup?"

Our heroine looks Nepomuk directly into his eyes and smiles as he takes her plate and returns to the kitchen for second helpings.

"I'm not interested in reputation or immortality or things like that," Nepomuk shouts. "I don't care what I'm remembered for. I don't care if I'm remembered. I don't care if I'm not remembered. I don't care why I'm remembered. I genuinely don't care."

Nepomuk returns from the kitchen. The soup steams. He places the plate in front of our heroine.

"We're living with bad surroundings. Don't you think?" our heroine says.

"In individuals, insanity is rare. But in groups and parties and nations and epochs it is the rule," Nepomuk answers. "The lie is a condition of life. Success has always been a great liar. We've always been living with bad surroundings. Our demons have not disappeared. They've merely got new names. But chance is everywhere. Even if some people blow up the world, and all they feel is sorry for themselves. However, whoever fights monsters should see to it that in the process he does not become a monster. Because if you gaze long enough into an abyss, the abyss will gaze back into you."

Nepomuk pauses and after a moment of silence continues to say: "You know, the salvation of the world consists in the salvation of the individual soul. He who has a why to live can bear almost any how. There are various truths, and as a result there is no truth. You have your way. I have my way. As for the right way, the correct way, and the only way, it does not exist. But the defeats are also battles. Because truth will triumph."

Our heroine nods.

"Truth will triumph," she repeats as Nepomuk's house begins to tremble and the floor begins to shake like jello.

Nepomuk twitches.

Our heroine doesn't even notice the earthquake that's hitting Ecuador.

Rabbi Nepomuk Glass remarks his guest's apathy to the natural disaster.

"Did you know that dark matter is undetectable?" our heroine asks.

"No, I did not," Nepomuk answers.

"But its presence has great gravitational effects," she says.

"I see. It's gonna be a very dangerous season," Nepomuk concludes.

Our heroine, the ravishing girl with Hershey's chocolate bar skin who has already killed three men in cold blood and with full intent, slightly nods her head.

It's 6.58.37 P.M. as...

...the earthquake with a 7.8 magnitude strikes the coast of Ecuador. Tremors are felt in neighboring Colombia and Peru. At least 700 people are killed and more than 30.000 injured.

In Guayaquil - approximately 190 miles from the epicenter - an overpass collapses on a car, killing the driver. A state of emergency is declared.

The earthquake is followed by over 55 aftershocks in the first 24 hours.

¡Me cago en la leche!

Part Two

1.

A few days later. Wednesday, April 20, 2016. 8 P.M. The Guayaquil City Hall. Deputy Mayor Ilcamaria Fiorela von Buchwald presses her right hand against her office window. She looks straight at the most emblematic statue of the city. The Simon Bolivar and San Martin monument.

Deputy Mayor von Buchwald is in her late forties as well and in tremendous physical shape. (Well, she's had bulimia and anorexia since she was 15. Why? We'll find out later.) For the moment this is what's important: Deputy Mayor Ilcamaria Firorela von Buchwald is non-negotiable, a woman without conscience or morale. Her line is the one of pressure, deceit, of greedy mercantilism. A genuine picture book lawmaker with the lips of Marilyn Monroe and the eyes of Caligula.

Von Buchwald treats her staff the way Alfred Hitchcock treated blondes. If you're new at the game and an inexperienced Tippi Hedren, you can effortlessly be made to squirm. More pro aides can expect to be treated like Grace Kelly.

Three of von Buchwald's little helpers, two women and one man, are presently in her somber and archetypically furnished office.

Big desk *de mierda*.

Big Ecuadorian flag *de mierda*.

Big Guayaquil flag de mierda.

Big photographs *de mierda* of her with celebrities *de mierda* and business heavyweights *de mierda*.

It smells like big money *de mierda* and big ego *de mierda*.

This *perra* is a power pussy.

"Some go out to fleece and come back sheared," she says. "The idle remarks of the rich are taken as maxims of wisdom by the poor. Those people never learn."

Von Buchwald turns around and looks at her aides. All eyes are glued on the television set. Footage of the government having difficulties distributing food and water to people in need after the earthquake in the coastal provinces of the country.

Women dally in tents.

Children cry.

Men shake their fists in anger.

It's miserable.

Despite the good will.

Despite international help.

Despite the fact that the government has raised taxes to pay for the those in need.

But where's the money?

Other than deep in the pockets of needy politicians like...

¿Qué te parece?

"This could be the most devastating disaster since the 1949 Ambato earthquake. President Rafael Correa...," the TC Television reporter Debbie Benites begins.

Aide 1 passes a nervous hand over her eyes.

"Oh, my God," she says.

"They're gonna be fine," aide 2 says. "Remember Tumaco in 1979?"

"Oh, yeah," aide 3 says as von Buchwald turns off the television set.

"Enough," she says. "When the legend becomes fact, print the legend. Now, back to business. Our campaign is about more than replacing the Mayor. It's about saving the soul of our country. You run Guayaquil. You run Ecuador. I'm Deputy Mayor. And I'm always responsible. Not the bloody Mayor. And Correa will be history soon. We'll build him a monument. Make him a legend. *Dios, patria y libertad.*"

"Precisely, Deputy Mayor," aide 2 says.

"Good," von Buchwald continues. "Now. I dashed in late in the game. I was the underdog. I pocketed my endorsements. The people crowned their Cinderella. It wasn't me. Why? Because voters, 'regular folks', have always been like a little kid in an ice cream store. Always distracted by the flavor of the month. Democracy in a nation of 15 million can be noisy and messy and complicated. That won't change tonight, and it shouldn't."

The aides snicker.

"Now," von Buchwald continues. "Today I've extra clout and I know only an angry voter's a good voter. I don't need to make nicey-nice to court my supporters and keep him from running. I can't not engage. I cannot retreat."

"Him? Who?" aide 1 asks as von Buchwald reacts confused.

"Did I say him?" she asks.

The aides quickly exchange glances.

"Oh, you mean him," aide 1 says.

"What I understood was that, for better or worse, history was turned topsy-turvey that night for our country," aide 2 whispers to aide 3 as von Buchwald gets promptly back on track.

"It was a tragedy," she says, "an act of God. Now. What we need to figure out, what we need to focus on, is who is in demand by the grassroots? Who is in demand by the media? We need to move towards the center, towards the women."

"In all my political experience," aide 2 says, "I don't even recall the women vote swinging a close election. The other side..."

Von Buchwald throws her the GK look first followed by the TH look.

"Let's talk about our intentions," she says. "I don't want to be the leader who built empires. Or sought grandeur. Or extended dominion. I want to be the leader who educated young children. Who helped to feed the hungry. Who helped the poor to find their way and who protected the right of every citizen to vote in every election. If you let a bully come in your front yard, he'll be on your porch the next day and the day after he'll rape your wife in your own bed. We don't oppose anybody per se for what God made them, they have a fight to their own identity as much as we do. All we want to do is to preserve the ethnic and cultural identity of our people. We want the same human rights as everyone else."

The aides nod and von Buchwald confirms her chauvinism: "Every form of life on this planet is beautiful and must be preserved. Oh, I've been itching for the fight for months. I don't wanna be flashy. But I don't wanna come across as foolish either. I wanna be the last man standing."
She laughs and continues: "Last woman standing. Of course."

Aide 1 chuckles.

¡El lameculos!

"Most importantly," von Buchwald says, "and I suppose you all know this, I don't look too good on the second row of our City Hall. This time around, this time I wanna win that second slipper. If you know what I mean."

The aides applaud as aide 3 gets very enthused.

"Yeah," she screams as the door to the office opens and...

...our heroine enters.

She's dressed in a black A-Line skirt, low heals, white blouse. (Think Sonia Rykiel or Rei Kawakubo.). Our heroine looks camera-ready while the others resemble boys at a Bar Mitzvah.

"Let's keep our personal ambitions in check, shall we," von Buchwald orders as aide 3 cools down.

"Of course," she says. "You must talk about repairing the nation, Deputy Mayor, about repairing the continent. Believe in Ecuador. Believe in..."

Von Buchwald throws him the GK look.

"How about a March on Quito?" aide 1 suggests.

"A March on Quito?" von Buchwald asks.

"Like in America," aide 1 continues, "the March on Washington in 1963. The largest political rally for human rights in history. Martin Luther King. I have a dream..."

Von Buchwald throws her the TH look.

"No? How about a march on Rome? Like in 1922. Mussolini?" aide 1 asks.

"We need a slogan. Something unforgettable, catchy, sexy," aide 2 interrupts.

Von Buchwald throws her the GK look.

"Load. Cock. Aim. Fire," aide 2 says facetiously.

Von Buchwald throws her the TH look.

"Equal but different?" aide 1 suggests carefully.

They all throw her the TH look as our heroine opens the door and is about to leave.

"Truth will triumph," she says.

Everybody stares at her.

¡Silencio!

"What did you say?" von Buchwald asks.

"I said, truth will triumph," our heroine answers. "That's what I said. Truth will triumph. Is there anything else you need, Deputy Mayor?"

"Truth will triumph," von Buchwald repeats and asks our heroine: "Who are you?"

"I'm a temp," our heroine answers.

"A temp?" von Buchwald repeats. "Say, temp, what's your job description? What exactly does a temp do?"

"Well," our heroine answers while standing still, "I find myself doing so many things these days that I've never done before."

Von Buchwald nods and smiles.

"Sounds like the good old days," she says. "You know, I did my best work when I was ignorant."

Her aides react threatened by our heroine and her uninhibited attitude that von Buchwald seems to value.

"Truth will triumph," she repeats, "that's good. That's really good."

"Thank you," our heroine says as she's about to leave again.

"A temp, remarkable," von Buchwald addresses her three aides. "Hold on, *niña*, what are you doing tonight?"

¿Niña?

¡Niña!

The aides are really pissed now. At all events, our heroine has no time to answer. Because suddenly the room experience a power outage caused by yet another aftershock.

Everything and everybody drown in perfect darkness. The aides start stumbling into things and each other.

They start cursing.

Stuff falls down and breaks.

Chaos.

"This is certainly a surprise," von Buchwald says as she somehow makes it across the room to our heroine.

"Let's continue our talk at my place, shall we?" she whispers to our heroine.

"You sure this is what you want?" our heroine whispers back to her.

"You'd do me a great favor," von Buchwald hisses. "And your country."

"There will be no miracles," our heroine says.

"We haven't promised any - yet," von Buchwald says as she touches our heroine's hand.

"Okay," our heroine decides.

Quickly von Buchwald and our heroine leave in silence as one of the aides light a match.

Everybody looks for von Buchwald.

"She's gone," aide 2 realizes.

"She always does things her way," aide 3 says.

¡La golfa!

"We should be pretty happy that we work here," aide 1 says. "I don't know why you aren't grateful. And by the way, I don't like your profanities."

The two aides throw her the TH look as the match dies and the three are back in utter blackness.

"Ouch!" aide 1 screams, "who was that? Hey! You think that's funny? Cowards!"

Suddenly aide 1 hears as the door opens and closes again.

"Hello? Where are you? Don't leave me alone. Hey, we're a team, are we not?" she whispers as she runs into the door while...

...our heroine and Deputy Mayor von Buchwald are already in the back in von Buchwald's limousine driving towards her mansion in Samborondón. Traffic is slow and dense. Once again it's hot and humid. Von Buchwald pours herself a drink.

"This is my nation," she says. "And my nation's ill. But I'm an optimist. I wish success for my nation. Now. You probably think I'm the classic rental politician. You want to try it? Get in the ring."

Our heroine shakes her head. Von Buchwald smiles. She enjoys her lecture.

"It's really nice talking to you, *niña*," she says. "You know what I mean?"

¿Niña?

¡Niña!

"I don't think I do," our heroine says.

"I know you don't. Actually, I prefer talking to men. There's a streak of female curiosity, the cunts, who are nasty because you're another woman. It's very upsetting. I always feel when there's a stiletto knife hidden behind the back. You're different. Dignity does not come from avenging insults, especially with violence. Politics. It's like war. A racket. Occasionally it improves lives. But more often it leaves misery and squalor. We need to change. We can do better. Progress. Humanity. Truth is, I don't want to be another racketeer for big business. All gangsters for capitalism," von Buchwald says as she remarks our heroine's facial injuries.

"A bit of misfortune?" she asks.

Our heroine looks at herself in the window.

"I need to think about being more thoughtful," she says.

Von Buchwald nods as if she presumes that our heroine is a victim of domestic violence. No surprise.

¡Este es Guayaquil!

"You're not fooling me," von Buchwald says. "You're hurt. You're hurt bad. Sex clings to women like a skin. We're not like men per se, *niña.* A man would prefer to come home to an unmade bed and a happy woman than to a neatly made bed and an angry woman. Grumbling is the death of love. Hell, I don't want to be part of this politicized gentleman's club. Provoke, negotiate, rinse and repeat? Do I have a choice? Yes. Never underestimate the willingness of politicians to try to avoid making some of the tough choices. Although, but mostly, yes, mostly I'm just sort of a concierge. Or a temp. Just like you. Our days are numbered, though, *niña*!"

Von Buchwald laughs. She can hold her liquor, but the booze has loosened her tongue.

"I talk too much, don't I?" she asks as our heroine smiles kindly.

Von Buchwald continues with her self-fulfilling prophecy.

"When I stop talking," she says, "you'll know I'm dead."

Our heroine looks at von Buchwald who downs her drink and pours herself a second beverage. Johnny Walker Black Label.

"Now," she says, "they always say I'm anti this and anti that. Let me ask you, is it ethical, is it moral to rent out an air mattress borrowed from a friend?"

Our heroine looks at von Buchwald.

"For 100$, I am willing to table the question," von Buchwald continues.

She laughs but our heroine doesn't.

"See," von Buchwald says, "how quickly things are not so black and white any longer. Believe me, two tits are mightier than two wagons."

Suddenly the limousine stops brusquely. Our heroine catapults forward. Von Buchwald clutches her with her right arm, while elegantly balancing her drink, which is still in her left hand. Our heroine's startled. Von Buchwald leaves her arm around our heroine's waist. She enjoys how her guest feels like. Our heroine hates every second of it. And von Buchwald knows better. She releases our heroine who sits back down just as the drive continues. Von Buchwald smiles at our heroine and finishes her drink.

"You okay?" she asks.

Our heroine nods. In need of fresh air, von Buchwald opens her window. The noise of the city pours inside the car. Von Buchwald quickly closes the window and continues to take the floor while our heroine listens attentively.

"What do I want?" von Buchwald asks. "What do I want? I just want a normal country, normal and modern. If that's a drawback, if that's my weakness, so be it. I'm curious. What's a temp's destiny?"

"Perhaps being without a destiny is my weakness," our heroine answers. "Temporarily."

Von Buchwald reacts rather surprised as the limousine enters the gate to her magnificent hacienda in Samborondòn...

...where von Buchwald and our heroine place themselves in the library and begin to work on von Buchwald's campaign.

"Read it again," she asks as our heroine writes 'the desire to escape every personal responsibility' on a legal pad.

Candles are lit. A tray with *empanadas* rests on the wooden floor. Two empty bottles of wine attest to the ambiance. A third bottle's already half-empty.

Von Buchwald looks at our heroine with mock-puzzled amusement as she follows her orders: "It's the worst in us which is being systematically activated and enlarged. Egotism, hypocrisy, indifference, cowardice, fear, resignation, and the desire to escape every personal responsibility."

Our heroine glances at von Buchwald who appears to be satisfied.

"I couldn't have said it better myself. A killer speech. Thank you," von Buchwald says. "How about a little break."

Our heroine puts the legal pad down. Von Buchwald moves her neck from side to side and pours herself a glass of red wine.

"It's not true that you shouldn't drink alone," she says. "These can be the happiest glasses you ever drain. Tonight, however, thanks to you, I'm not alone. When you've worked hard and done well and walked through that doorway of opportunity, you do not slam the door shut behind you."

"Are you married, Deputy Mayor?" our heroine changes the subject.

"Call me Ilcamaria, dear," von Buchwald offers. "Yes, I'm married to the people and their fate."

Von Buchwald seems surprised by her own response. Dead serious she continues: "No. I cannot marry. I must not. I won't replace our founding principles. I will reapply them. I like to come in first. There's nothing wrong with that."

"You don't miss it, love?" our heroine continues to ask.

"Love?", von Buchwald says. "At my age? When you're 21 all you want is find true love at the San Marino shopping mall. I should say that the best definition of love is you're with the person you want to hold your hand when you die. And I don't say that. They'll love me. They'll die to love me, my people. You'll see."

"You don't miss having kids?" our heroine wants to know.

"Kids?" von Buchwald laughs. "Children? No. Absolutely not. I'm so happy that I didn't have any. But I can appreciate that earth-mother thing, feeding the masses. The only thing that matters is the unification of the people, and all the other people don't matter. What do you think?"

Our heroine doesn't respond.

"Plus," von Buchwald continues, "I'd be afraid my kids getting fiddled by queer priests and twisted school-teachers. Fuck Humboldt!"

As concerns: Von Buchwald too went to the CAH. She too graduated in 1986. Was in love with her German teacher. Herr W. And Herr W. in lust with her. A lot. Ordered to perform oral sex on him, raped her anally. Called her *kleine Fotze* and eventually popped her cherry.

At first von Buchwald's whole life was shaken. Her dreams were corrupted by the school. She was never going to be the same, stripped of her dignity and confidence. Even worse: No one intervened on her behalf because her tormentor was supported by an eminent, trustworthy and celebrated institution.

Poor girl became ill. (Hence the eating disorders.) Until she discovered politics for herself. Realized that sensitive people are just tyrannical people; everybody else has to adapt to them. Decided to take the law into her own hands and with a little help of her friends made sure that Herr W. never touched nobody again.

"My God, these feeling types. This nation's gotta change. But you, you look like a person that likes children," von Buchwald continues.

Our heroine keeps her poker face.

"Can I ask you a personal question, Deputy Mayor?" she asks.

"Ilcamaria," von Buchwald says.

"Ilcamaria," our heroine agrees.

"Shoot," von Buchwald says.

"You miss intimacy?" our heroine asks.

Von Buchwald smiles and gets up. She shuffles to our heroine who sits on a sofa and places herself on the floor in front of her. Our heroine looks at the back of von Buchwald's head.

"Intimacy. Loyalty. Both make betrayal more likely," von Buchwald says. "Take my two cents' worth. Nothing's more embarrassing than sincerity. Nothing."

Von Buchwald looks behind herself into our heroine's face. Their eyes lock.

"Would you mind?" von Buchwald asks. "It's been a hard day."

Our heroine understands as von Buchwald turns her head around and bows it. Our heroine puts her hands on von Buchwald's neck. She begins rubbing it. Von Buchwald enjoys the massage. A lot! In fact, it really turns her own. Von Buchwald begins to moan. Her hairless pussy's already dripping wet before she can even take her Princess tam-tam G-string off.

"It's getting hot in here," she whispers. "Open the door, will you."

Our heroine gets up. She opens the door to the terrace and looks outside. It's raining. Finally. Our heroine goes back to the sofa.

Meanwhile von Buchwald has liberated herself from her bra. She's flaunting the rosy peaks of her nipples that are visible through the beige silk blouse. Von Buchwald smiles at our heroine who sits back down on the sofa and continues with the massage as von Buchwald gets more raunchy, now fingering herself. There's no way back...

"Truth will triumph," von Buchwald sighs. "You're so good with words. I want you to join my team. In fact, you'll be the team. Those imbeciles. All they do is talk shit to my ear and blow smoke up my ass. I've come too far to turn back now. Longevity, that's what it's all about. I trust you."

"Gato escaldodo del agua fria huye," our heroine says.

"Once bitten, twice shy. You sound like me", von Buchwald says.

"On the other hand, I like to do things for which I'm unqualified," our heroine responds.

Von Buchwald, now deliciously excited, laughs as her panties move off of her. She's spreading her legs and begins to rub her epic clit.

"Building a state can be hard work," our heroine continues.

"You bet it is, *niña,*" von Buchwald moans.

¡Niña!

"That's what my husband used to say," our heroine says.

Von Buchwald raises her head a tiny bit.

"That building a state is hard work," our heroine says.

"He changed his mind?" she asks.

Our heroine takes von Buchwald's hand and kisses it.

"No," she says. "He died."

Von Buchwald reacts surprised.

"He was murdered," our heroine says.

"That's awful," von Buchwald says. "Who killed him?"

"You did, Deputy Mayor", our heroine says. "You did."

Our heroine's response unbalances von Buchwald. She turns her head around and looks straight into our heroine's eyes. Von Buchwald's eyes reflect acknowledgement and recollection. But she's still super-hot, like our heroine has lit a bonfire inside of her snatch.

"The trouble with a mask is it never changes," our heroine says.

"Yeah," von Buchwald wails. "But look, a girl's got to do something for a living these days. I prefer to review things my way."

Our heroine continues to kiss von Buchwald's hand and to suck her fingers as von Buchwald continues to fondle herself.

"Fair enough," our heroine says. "You can create many worlds for yourself. But you need to share them. With me."

Deputy Mayor von Buchwald, however, does not want to share anything. She refuses the second chance granted by our heroine. Just like all the others before her.

"We're like the Phoenix," von Buchwald sighs. "Always rising from the ashes. I wake up every morning in a house that was built by slaves. I'm going to continue to stand with the people that are being oppressed. You think you're superior to me?"

"No," our heroine says, "you've got nicer hands."

"Call me butterfingers. I use cosmetic fluids. And egg oil," von Buchwald reveals. "Well, my arms need some serious toning, though. I like your legs better."

"The legs aren't so beautiful. I just know what to do with them," our heroine says as she presses her legs against von Buchwald's shoulders who smiles contentedly and now weeps a little. She pushes her head against our heroine's groin.

"Tomorrow I'll be walking funny," von Buchwald gripes. "Now, my young apprentice. Only a few people are above the law. Because they are the law. Sometimes life doesn't leave you many choices. He was in the wrong place. You're in the right place. Hey, it's always either victory..."

Out of the blue our heroine grabs von Buchwald's head, twists it and quickly breaks her neck.

"...or death," our heroine finishes von Buchwald's sentence while the Deputy Mayor's spiritless head is at anchor in her lap.

"The door is closed for good. You won't be walking anywhere tomorrow," our heroine says as she senses some sort of danger.

She's right.

¡Mierda!

She spots an Ecuadorian Coral Snake which is one of South America's most venomous reptiles also known as 20-minute-snake for the victim is supposed to be dead within 20 minutes after being bitten by one. It slithers directly towards our heroine who is entrapped by von Buchwald's dead body...

...as Nepomuk makes himself comfortable in his recliner chair reading Rilke's *Book of Hours*. On his gramophone turns a record. It's Bach's St. Matthew Passion.

Less than 20 minutes into the recording there's a knock on his door. Nepomuk doesn't pay attention to the noise. He's totally immersed in the literature and the music.

Someone knocks again. This time with more verve.

Nepomuk hears the sound and gets up. He's hunched over like the victim of a whipping. He walks slowly to the door and opens it and sees...

...our heroine.

She's soaking wet, pale as a ghost, her body shudders.

Before Nepomuk can say anything, our heroine collapses.

After a moment of hesitation, Nepomuk lifts her off the floor and carries our heroine into his apartment.

¡Hostia puta!

Time's ticking...

Only a few hours later Lieutenant Ortega Revelo and Major Sanchez Zamora walk through the garden of von Buchwald's hacienda.

"You v- v- v-ote for her?" Lieutenant Ortega Revelo asks as Major Sanchez Zamora blows his nose and quickly continues: "I never v- v- v-oted because I was never sure it was for r- r- r-eal."

Major Sanchez Zamora cleans his nose.

"Like, after cha- cha- cha-nges," Lieutenant Ortega Revelo says, "you know, they're all th- th- th-e same."

Major Sanchez Zamora folds his handkerchief ignoring his partner's thoughts. Instead, he continues to eat his *Bolon de Verde,* a green plantain dumpling stuffed with cheese.

"Not a sparrow falls that God does not know," he proclaims. "Thank you, Ilcamaria Fiorela. Give peace a chance."

Lieutenant Ortega Revelo looks at his boss and shakes his head. He's startled that his patron knew the Deputy Mayor.

Before Lieutenant Ortega Revelo can ask any questions, Major Sanchez Zamora says: "She was legendary. You know why?"

Lieutenant Ortega Revelo shrugs.

"Darling Ilcamaria," Major Sanchez Zamora says, "sought to salvage our nation. She was like an engineer rebuilding a bridge. She knew she could not demolish it, since that would disrupt traffic. So, she began to do what? She replaced each individual part and passengers wouldn't even notice. She was a genius. And a saint. You know, the practical reason for freedom is that freedom seems to be the only condition under which any kind of substantial moral fiber can be developed. Everything else has been tried, world without end. Going dead against reason and experience, we have tried law, compulsion and authoritarianism of various kinds, and the result is nothing to be proud of."

Lieutenant Ortega Revelo isn't impressed. He's top to bottom apolitical.

"With all due r- r- r-espect, patron," he says, "it's t- t- t-wo in the morning, and the lady of ch- ch- ch-ange is toast."

Major Sanchez Zamora throws him the MD look.

"Many years ago, Lieutenant, we made sure that no one would ever touch her again. But tonight...," he says as they arrive in the middle of von Buchwald's library. Her dead body leans against the sofa. The middle finger of her right hand still sticks deep in her clean-shaven vagina.

"If Muhammad does not go to the mountain, the mountain will go to Muhammad," a sinister looking cop says. "The dream-team. Lieutenant Laurel and Captain Hardy."

A second cop, likewise smug, approaches Major Sanchez Zamora and Lieutenant Ortega Revelo and says: "Shouldn't you be kinda busy on your reservation, boys?"

"E- e- e-veryhing's under co- co- co-ntrol," Lieutenant Ortega Revelo says as the cops start laughing and begin to ape him and his cleft lip.

Lieutenant Ortega Revelo reacts embarrassed.

"Hey, Sanchez. Ever thought about going on a diet?" the first cop asks as Major Sanchez Zamora grins wickedly. Like MD on drugs.

Nobody fucks with him or his partner.

¡Nadie!

Major Sanchez Zamora jumps forward like a massive hippo. He grabs one of the cops by the throat, stuffs the rest of the *Bolon de Verde* in his mouth and lifts him up. Like a puppet.

"It's Major Sanchez Zamora, you louse. And I weigh too much 'cause I eat too much. I eat some bad things too. I like my *Bolon de Verde* for breakfast. Sometimes I eat two. Occasionally three. But rarely," he says.

"To hell with lean cuisine. I got started right this morning with *Patacones*. I'll tell ya, almost as delicious as my *Bolon de Verde*. Talk to me!"

The cop can hardly breathe while the other one is too shocked to react.

"I'm not in the habit of warning more than once," Major Sanchez Zamora adds as he peels the rest of the *Bolon de Verde* out of the cop's mouth.

"Door was open. Neighbor found the Deputy Mayor. She had left her office with a temp. Her aides told us," the cop says semi-conscious.

Now Lieutenant Ortega Revelo speaks up.

"Tell us so- so- so-mething we don't kn- kn- know," he demands

"She was pretty, the temp was a real *niña*," the cop mumbles.

"How pretty?" Lieutenant Ortega Revelo continues. "Nice pretty or cour- cour- cour-tsey-on-my-face-pretty?"

Major Sanchez Zamora grins. His sidekick's not so goody two-shoes after all.

"She was a slippery, angry, black bitch! My Lord, she was blessed with beauty! She'll probably eat your face," the cop coughs as Lieutenant Ortega Revelo jumps into the air and Major Sanchez Zamora drops the cop on the floor.

The cop rips his collar open trying to catch more air and spits the rest of the *Bolon de Verde* out. His speechless colleague helps him.

"¡Caramba!" Lieutenant Ortega Revelo screams. "Watch out, little *niña*!"

Only a second later he reveals to Major Sanchez Zamora: "Sorry, *pa- pa- pa-tron* that I lost the gun. We could've saved your friend."

¡Fue una mierda!

"Lieutenant," Major Sanchez Zamora whispers in his year, "between us, there are things we do but do not mention. *Bueno*?"

Lieutenant Ortega Revelo nods as Major Sanchez Zamora gives him a friendly pat on the shoulder: "Don't worry about it. Julia Child was just shy of 50 when she wrote her first cookbook. With your talent, you'll catch on in no time."

"Thank you," Lieutenant Ortega Revelo says not knowing who the fuck Julia Child is as Major Sanchez Zamora points at the tray with the *empanadas*.

"You processed those?" he asks the cops.

They nod in silence as Major Sanchez Zamora walks to the tray. He bends over it and chooses an *empanada* with chicken.

For a brief moment, Lieutenant Ortega Revelo sees his back up weapon. It's a NAA Mini Revolver which rests in an ankle holster.

Major Sanchez Zamora marks a puddle of dried blood next to the tray. He checks von Buchwald's legs. No injuries. He glimpses under the sofa and spots the snake.

Their eyes lock.

The petrified reptile withdrawals.

Major Sanchez Zamora takes a big bite from the *empanada*.

"The universe does care about us," he says full of delight as he turns around and faces Lieutenant Ortega Revelo. "She's on the tip of my tongue."

Meanwhile, she shivers in Nepomuk's bed.

She's in a delirium.

She has very high temperature. Nepomuk's wiping sweat from her forehead.

She twists and turns.

"Don't. Don't hurt him," she mumbles. "Don't hurt my husband. No. Please. He hasn't done anything. Let him go, please. He's everything, I've got. Please, take me. I love him so much. Kill me, kill me, let him live. Please!"

Nepomuk's trying his best to calm her down as...

...Major Sanchez Zamora and Lieutenant Ortega Revelo wait at the cash register of a neighborhood shop.

The cashier, a very homely girl with loads and loads of spots on her uneven face, looks at the items: four packs of Nicorette stop smoking gum, several candy bars and...

...she stops at a ¡Hola! magazine with former Miss Colombia Ariadna Gutiérrez on the cover.

"She's so pretty," the cashier says with a sigh.

"And so are you, *niña,*" Major Sanchez Zamora says absolutely sincere. "If people are happy and blissful within, if they're filled with universal love within, they don't have any desire to hurt anyone or make violence. They just enjoy life and enjoy all the diversity in life."

The cashier blushes. She smiles and shows her braces. Major Sanchez Zamore kisses her cheek.

Lieutenant Ortega Revelo glances at him - indifferently.

"Look, Lieutenant," Major Sanchez Zamora says on their way out, "carry out a random act of kindness, with no expectation of reward, safe in the knowledge that one day someone might do the same for you."

Lieutenant Ortega Revelo looks puzzled.

"Will you do that for me one day?" Major Sanchez Zamora asks. "Will you carry us a random act of kindness?"

"Of course, *pa- pa- pa-tron*, of course," Lieutenant Ortega Revelo answers.

"Good," Major Sanchez Zamora says. "Words can sometimes, in moments of grace, attain the quality of deeds. There is nothing more important than appearing to be human."

A week later. Wednesday, April 27, 2016. Our heroine's finally waking up in Nepomuk's bedroom. She doesn't know where she is. From the adjoining living room someone's shouting in a language that seems utterly strange to her.

Our heroine slowly rises and leaves the bed. As she enters the living room, she sees Nepomuk who sits in the recliner chair watching the tube.

The voice is coming from the TV. History channel. It's Adolf Hitler who's giving a speech. Our heroine doesn't know him. She's even more confused now.

The program shows AH in front of a huge crowd. The men and women all go apeshit.

¿Qué demonios...?

"Who is he?" our heroine asks.

Nepomuk now notices our heroine who stands behind him. She's wearing his striped pyjamas.

"A ghost," Nepomuk says. "How're you?"

He turns off the television. Still weak from the snakebite, our heroine sits down.

"Did your daughter come?" she asks.

"No," Nepomuk says. "How're you?"

"I don't know," our heroine answers. "How long..."

"A week," Nepomuk says. "I'm sorry about the TV."

Our heroine looks at the television.

"What's going on?" she asks. "What was that?"

"That was Germany," Nepomuk says.

"Where you were born?" our heroine asks.

Nepomuk nods.

"Tell me," our heroine demands.

"Tell you what?" Nepomuk asks.

"Tell me about Germany, Nepo," our heroine says.

"Tell you about Germany," Nepomuk repeats. "Well, one day we build beautiful architecture, the next Auschwitz."

"Auschwitz," our heroine says. "And what is Auschwitz?"

Nepomuk thinks.

How can he explain Auschwitz to our heroine?

"My father," Nepomuk begins. "My father. He's smoking. Flicking ashes out of the window. He has said nothing. Finally crushes the cigarette in the dashboard ashtray and turns to me. 'Son,' he says, 'son, I want to say something to you. I'm only going to say it once, and I don't want you asking me any questions. Okay? You read the papers. You know what's going on. I may not come home one of these nights. I might have to go somewhere else. If that happens, I'm going to depend on you to take my place with Mom.' He didn't say anything else. Neither did I. We must've driven the rest of the way home in silence. I do remember very distinctly what I felt. Fear.

Despite all the talk, I had believed that my father and his friends would protect us from it."

Nepomuk pauses for an instant then he continues to say: "I never had a balloon burst. I never fell off a bike and skinned my knee. My parents never forced me to conjugate or to keep quiet during lunch or dinner. They never made me take baths or tidy my room. I was never bullied by my older brothers or teased by my sisters. And I never had a quarter roll with weary deliberation down a grate. What luck. That's Auschwitz."

Silence.

Our heroine nods.

"The Germans did this?" she asks.

Nepomuk nods. His eyes mirror the pain that's been locked inside of him for a lifetime.

"But you're German," our heroine states.

Nepomuk nods again.

"Oh, Germany," he says. "Where nothing changes! If you prick us, do we not bleed? If you tickle us, do we not laugh? If you poison us, do we not die?"

"And if you wrong us," our heroine says, "shall we not revenge?"

Nepomuk shrugs.

"The tears I've cried over Germany have dried. I've washed my face," he says.

"What about your family?" our heroine asks.

"I'm one person only," Nepomuk answers. "I never mentioned it to anybody. Not ever. I don't think it's the kind of thing to be telling to anybody. Not what I saw. But you know, according to a Talmudic parable, all Jews, past, present and future, were there at the foot of Sinai; in a certain sense, all were present at Auschwitz. So perhaps I'm not so alone after all. The necessity and impossibility of being a Jew."

"You were a child. It wasn't your fault," our heroine says.

"That doesn't make it less painful," Nepomuk answers.

"That's why you became a rabbi?" our heroine asks.

"No," Nepomuk says. "Failure as an atheist."

Our heroine nods.

"I am precisely what I am not, because I did not exist until I became it, above all else: a Jew," Nepomuk says.

"Let's say," she says, "let's suppose you could..."

Nepomuk smiles and rises. Slowly he walks to one of his bookshelves and gets a thick ring binder. He brings it to our heroine and hands it to her. Our heroine opens the folder. She looks at newspaper clippings and pictures of a man in a Waffen-SS uniform. Nepomuk points at the folder.

"Lipschis," he says, "Name's Hans Lipschis. He said he was just a cook. But he wasn't just a cook."

"Why did he hate you?" our heroine asks.

"He didn't hate me," Nepomuk answers. "He just did his job. They all did."

"Is he dead?" our heroine asks.

"He was hiding in the US but was deported back to Germany. That's where he lives. *In der Heimat*," Nepomuk says.

Our heroine looks at him. She didn't understand the last sentence.

"In the homeland, my homeland," Nepomuk clarifies.

"You don't wanna go over there and look him up?" our heroine suggests.

"Do I want to look Hans Lipschis up?" Nepomuk asks. "Listen, not every bridge wants to be crossed."

Our heroine doesn't believe Nepomuk.

"Are you sure," she says.

"My role is to maintain peace. I'm the master of my fate," he says.

Our heroine looks intensely at Nepomuk.

"But not the captain of your soul," she says.

"The past is never a justification, only a poor excuse. It confers no right, and rights no wrongs. It's even more heartless than..."

"God?" our heroine interrupts.

"Sometimes silence is the ideal solution to a problem," Nepomuk says.

Our heroine looks at her hands holding the ring binder.

"These hands cannot be finished," she says.

"Really?" Nepomuk asks.

"We owe it to them, to their lives," our heroine says.

"I'm alive. And my life is my only talent. I'm not a victim. I am victory. *Schluß*," he says.

Nepomuk puts on his coat, takes his hat and his knapsack.

"I've got to go. My people are waiting," he says.

"Friday Night Out," our heroine says sarcastically.

Nepomuk ignores her cattily tone.

"Will you be there when I come back?" he asks.

Our heroine looks straight into Nepomuk's eyes.

"Did you save my life, rabbi?" she asks.

"No," Nepomuk says and walks over to the Santa Ana Hill Chapel...

...where he enters the nave.

Hundreds of people tarry in the aisles, on the pews and the transept.

Men, women and children, seeking refuge from the earthquake. Nepomuk's blown away. He's never seen the church so jammed.

Nepomuk strides to the chancel and climbs up the altar. This could be his day, his moment of validation. At last, Nepomuk's facing a vast audience that needs his console, his support and consequently God's words.

What does it matter that he's a rabbi and not a priest?

The faces stare at Nepomuk in outright silence. A woman's nursing her baby. An elderly couple's holding hands. Two girls are playing with their dolls. All taking in Nepomuk, all waiting for him to speak.

Nepomuk takes a big breath...

...then he surprises himself more than anybody else.

"I'm a stranger among strangers," he says and bows his head in defeat.

Nepomuk descends from the altar. He exits the church through the center aisle. The eyes of the coerced congregation follow him.

When he arrives back home...

...our heroine's gone.

Nepomuk opens the door to his bedroom. The bed has been properly made. He walks into the kitchen and opens the cabinet looking for something which he eventually finds. It's a sealed bottle of Bombay Sapphire Gin.

"Na, alter Freund. Alles klar?" Nepomuk addresses the bottle in German.

He grabs his old friend, a shot glass and slowly walks back into the living room where he sits down in his recliner chair. He stares at the bottle of booze in his hand.

"But I had to recognize and accept that my soul is a child and that my God in my soul is a child," he says to himself. "Be happy for this moment. This moment is your life."

Be that as it may, Nepomuk doesn't know what to do: To drink or not to drink. Someone else, however, has already made his decision...

...at round about the same time. The Bar 234 at Imbabura 234 near the Malecón Simón Bolivar. A man's on his knees vomiting into a loo and is very loud in doing so.

When he's done, he flushes the toilet and gets up. He steps out of the stall. Two young women stare at him. They're grossed out. The man realizes that he's in the ladies' room and shakes his head. He walks to the basin and looks into the mirror.

"Just gimme a pair of loose-fittin' shoes, some tight pussy, and a warm place to shit, an' ah'll be all right," the man who goes by the name Tusker says with the drawn-out drawl of a Texan accent.

His CV: A few years back Tusker was a real photographer. Today's he's merely a middle-aged forgotten barfly fighting his demons. Yet girls are suckered by his lazuli eyes and ruffle-me hair. Tusker is a character who does triple shots of intensity spiked with the vermouth of charm. He plays people like a Stradivarius, lets them slide inch by inch behind the mask of handsome, to hit upon a soul so shallow and petty that love must suffocate in it. Born and raised in Ecuador where his parents, both from Houston, Texas, worked as aid-workers.

(Tusker's father: "NGOs are in the business of selling bullshit for a living." Tusker's mother: "The first heap of cow dung is usually wrapped well and sold to the founders who are mostly groups of bleeding-heart liberals, white, of course, with a Mother T. complex." Tusker's father: "The better your bullshit, the more the money." Tusker's mother: "Bullshit is the life blood of the system.")

Tusker too, surprise, surprise, went to the CAH and since he loved the climate and his friends for life in school, he stayed in the country.

¡Dios, patria y libertad!

Tusker washes his face. He then tries to remove a vomit stain from his shirt. He does not succeed, however, and gives up. He turns around and looks at the two very attractive girls who have been watching him. Tusker grins at them. They are totally sickened by him. Tusker wobbles out of the ladies' room and enters the bar proper.

It's jam-packed. *Ecuador Cadaver,* a local metal band, rocks the house. The audience goes bananas. Tusker manages to make it to one of the bars.

"Wild Turkey 101," he hollers at the barman who belts out: "Your blood will run a lawn mower. You've had your last call, Tusker."

Tusker stands up straight. Shoulders back, tummy in.

"I didn't hear anyone yell last call. How could I?" he says. "I was in your bathroom, barfing in your bidet."

"Go home, Tusker," the barman says. "Booze is not the answer."

"Yeah," Tusker answers. "But it sure helps to forget the question."

Tusker frowns and looks around.

"Where there's a swill, there's a sway," he says to himself as he spots another bar in the establishment.

Tusker grins wickedly and goes on his mission. He weaves through the party crowd and arrives at his destination. Here it's less crowded and much quieter.

Tusker wedges himself between two beautiful girls. Twins, actually. They're eating French fries. Tusker ignores the girls for now. Instead, he signals to the bartender to come over.

"Gimme something delicate, yet with an audacious bouquet," he whispers to him.

The bartender grins, mixes the bar's signature drink in a plastic cup and places it in front of Tusker who smiles from ear to ear. Like a schoolboy. The girls stare at him.

"It's called Cuba Libre, cowboy," the girls say in chorus. "It's desperately sweet."

Tusker picks up the cup and addresses it.

"Alas, something in common, fucking commie drink," he says and drinks and drinks and drinks...

"So handsome," the girls say. "So alone. So unjust..."

Tusker finishes the Cuba Libre and makes eye contact with bartender. No words necessary. The bartender nods.

"So astonish me," Tusker says to the girls.

"Are you a bad, bad, bad boy?" they ask in unison.

"Multitasking, ladies, happens to be my forte," Tusker answers.

"Oh, you're gonna burn in hell," the girls say. "We feel it deep inside of us."

"The devil picks up the tab every night, right?" Tusker asks as the girls laugh.

Tusker steals a few of their French fries.

"You like potato. I like potahto. We like French fries," Tusker says as he drowns the fries in ketchup.

He stuffs them in his mouth. A dab of ketchup besmirches his shirt. The bartender places the fresh Cuba Libre in front of him.

"Taste it!" Tusker tells the bartender.

The bartender sips and reflects.

"It's perfect," he says.

"Then why the fuck didn't you make it that way in the first place," Tusker asks. "Boy, they don't even drink like that in Houston."

Tusker laughs hysterically. The bartender leaves.

"Hold me and watch my drink," he says to the girls while chewing and laughing.

The girls appear to be muddled by his statement. Tusker realizes his mistake and tries once more: "Watch me and hold my drink!"

He hands the Cuba Libre to one of the girls. He then jumps on the bar where he does a perfectly top-notch handstand as...

...he eyes our heroine who stands in the midst of the crowd beholding Tusker.

Our heroine blends right in, looking like everybody else. Ripped jeans, thermal underwear, flannel shirt, Doc Martens boots.

Tusker's vision suddenly turns blurry, unfocused and fuzzy. He loses his balance and falls to the ground. The girls help him up.

"You okay?" they say. "You hurt?"

Tusker looks befuddled. His eyes search for our heroine in the distance. He can't find her. Tusker doesn't know what to think of his vision. Was it just his imagination or was she really there? Whatever it was, for now he blames it on the Cuba Libre and all the other mouth-watering drinks he's had tonight.

"I must've gotten gravity-challenged," he says to the girls. "Sorry, I'm in no condition to fuck."

The girls smile auspiciously.

"Let's go home, *gringo*," they say.

The girls carry Tusker out of the bar while he barks a few lines from *Adoracion*: "*Soñé ser tuyo y en mi efántenerte prese en mis brazos para siempre mia; pero nunca soñé que he de perderte que otro mortal la dicha soureia.*"

Our heroine watches them while finishing her Vitaminwater before going home...

...where she folds two letters and crams them into an envelope. Focused and determined, our heroine seals and then stuffs it into the back pocket of her trousers.

Our heroine grabs a large, blue plastic bag, in which all of her belongings are. There's no more personal stuff in the studio. Just a bed, a table and a chair. One last curtain time.

Our heroine opens the door, turns off the lights and exits to the street...

...as she tosses the plastic bag on a pile of trash and then eyes her Shady Lady motorbike.

She takes the keys and throws them on the pile of trash too.

Less than 15 minutes later she's arrived at Nepomuk's place. The door is unlocked...

...and enters the living room. Nepomuk's still seated in his recliner chair. He's sound asleep, so it seems. The bottle of Bombay Sapphire Gin stands by his feet. Our heroine looks at the bottle. It's closed. The seal has not been broken. Our heroine tiptoes through the room. She tries to be as quiet as possible.

Our heroine approaches one of Nepomuk's bookshelves. She hides the envelope behind Rilke's *Book of Hours*.

Our heroine turns around and sees that Nepomuk's not covered. She crosses to the bedroom, gets a comforter and tugs him in.

"Is it time to say goodbye?" he asks with his eyes being closed.

Our heroine smiles as Nepomuk opens his eyes.

"What else is there to say to anyone in this life?" she says as she touches Nepomuk's shoulder.

"Yeah," he answers.

Our heroine turns around and approaches the door.

"Maybe it's true," Nepomuk begins as our heroine stops. "Maybe the way to glory leads through shame. I feel hate, but want to speak love. What does that make me?"

"I speak love, but use daggers. What does that make me?" our heroine answers.

Nepomuk reacts.

"Let's say," he says, "let's suppose I'd go to Germany and, you know, what then?"

"What then?" our heroine answers. "You'll cross that bridge when you get to it, Nepo."

Our heroine opens the door.

"To leave is to die a little, don't you think?" Nepomuk says.

Tears roll down our heroine's face.

"Yeah," she says.

"Evil has no face," Nepomuk says.

Our heroine reacts.

"You're wrong, Nepo, it does," she says. "I've seen it."

Our heroine leaves the apartment while Nepomuk stays in his recliner chair. He's all alone again. In the darkness. Like in a tunnel where nobody turns the light on. For number 202422.

Thursday morning, April 28, 2016. The Club Guayas de Tiro y Aviación. A shooting range. Several bullets go straight through the 10 of a B-27 target. Light shines through the holes.

The shooter's Lieutenant Ortega Revelo. He's using a Glock 22 in caliber .40 S&W.

Lieutenant Ortega Revelo flips a switch and the target comes back to him. He looks at the silhouette. Lieutenant Ortega Revelo's shot a perfect score. Major Sanchez Zamora's impressed.

"Actually," Lieutenant Ortega Revelo says without stammering, "I preferred the SIG Sauer 220 semi-automatic in caliber .45 ACP. Didn't you, *patron*?"

"You're a good gun, Lieutenant," Major Sanchez Zamora says. "We finally found something you're really good at."

"Thanks, *patron,*" Lieutenant Ortega Revelo says.

"What's your secret ingredient?" Major Sanchez Zamora asks.

"My shooting secret, you mean?" Lieutenant Ortega Zamora asks.

"Yeah, what's your shooting secret?" Major Sanchez Zamora repeats.

Lieutenant Ortega Zamora muses for an instant.

"Shooting's like making sweet love to your *niña, patron,*" he finally says. "Just gotta know when to hold your piece still."

Major Sanchez Zamora keeps quiet and then bursts out laughing. He bitch slaps Lieutenant Ortega Revelo as if they were best pals.

"Just gotta know when to hold your piece still," Major Sanchez Zamora repeats. "You and I, we'll have many more magic moments, my precious Gino Leandro."

Lieutenant Gino Leandro Ortega Revelo's full of cheer and feels accomplished. He hands the Glock to Major Sanchez Zamora who declines the pistol.

"Not now. Later," he says. "Scout's honor."

Lieutenant Ortega Revelo nods but appears to be disappointed.

"Let's go eat," Major Sanchez Zamora suggests. "I'm starved."

Major Sanchez Zamora leads the way.

"Sure, patron," Lieutenant Ortega Revelo says. "I meant to ask you..."

But Major Sanchez Zamora's gone. Lieutenant Ortega Revelo looks at the target and shrugs. He runs his fingers over the holes in the silhouette as our heroine's...

...talking on a public phone. Her gestures and facial expressions tell that she's giving orders. When our heroine's done, she dials a new number and waits...

...while Major Sanchez Zamora and Lieutenant Ortega Revelo are taking their car through the Medusa car wash at the Avenida de las Américas. Major Sanchez Zamora's behind the steering wheel. They are eating *Cuy* - guinea pig on a stick.

"This food," Lieutenant Ortega Revelo says, "doesn't taste right. Kosher salt. It's all about kosher salt."

Major Sanchez Zamora reacts surprised.

"Huh?" he says.

"I've been watching the Food Network," Lieutenant Ortega Revelo says. "The salt, you see, the salt isn't, like, kosher. It's just very pure so it can be used..."

"Lieutenant Ortega Revelo," Major Sanchez Zamora interrupts him.

"Yes," he says.

"What the fuck?" Major Sanchez Zamora says with a penetrating voice.

Lieutenant Ortega Revelo's confused by Major Sanchez Zamora's tone. Didn't he tell him to learn more about cooking? And wasn't he impressed by his shooting skills?

"It's, l-l- l-ike, I'm taking your advice. I'm learning how to coo- coo- coo-k," he says as his chutzpah dissolves like sugar in water.

"You're learning how to cook?" Major Sanchez Zamora repeats.

"You know," Lieutenant Ortega Revelo continues, "I'm getting ma- ma- ma-ried. I even read Julia Child's..."

"Married, Lieutenant Ortega Revelo?" Major Sanchez Zamora asks.

"Yeah," Lieutenant Ortega Revelo says full of joy.

"No shit!" Major Sanchez Zamora says.

"A marriage made in hea- hea- hea-ven," Lieutenant Ortega Revelo says.

"No, Lieutenant," Major Sanchez Zamora says. "That's thunder and lighting. There is always some madness in love. But there is always some reason in madness too."

Lieutenant Ortega Revelo smiles at his boss. He's too happy to be upset. He shows Major Sanchez Zamora a copy of Brides Magazine. Major Sanchez Zamora looks at a picture of a beautiful girl. She's wearing a gorgeous, white wedding gown.

"She'll look just l- l- l-ike that," Lieutenant Ortega Revelo explains. "Only better. Will you do me the honor and be my best man, *pa- pa- pa-tron*?"

Major Sanchez Zamora grabs the magazine and devours it with his MD eyes. Everything dawns on him, everything, everything, everything...

"I've been barking up the wrong tree, Lieutenant," he says.

Lieutenant Ortega Revelo doesn't understand.

Major Sanchez Zamora tosses the magazine at him and squeezes the hell out of the rest of his guinea pig as Lieutenant Ortega Revelo looks at *Brides Magazine*. He's totally astray.

"What the fu- fu- fu-ck?" Lieutenant Ortega Revelo says as Major Sanchez Zamora's cell phone rings.

He takes the call.

"Yeah?" he says.

"Talk to me, *pa- pa- pa-tron,*" Lieutenant Ortega Revelo begs.

Major Sanchez Zamora lifts his right index finger and says calmly: "Button up, Gino!"

Silencio.

Silencio absoluto.

Silencio muerto.

Dead silence.

It's as if time and space all at once stand still.

¡Hostia puta!

The water in the car wash suddenly changes to blood.

"¡Vete a la m- m- m-ierda!" Lieutenant Ortega Revelo shouts and makes the sign of the cross.

"You know where to find me?" our heroine says at the other end of the phone.

"Not many alternatives left, are there?" Major Sanchez Zamora says.

"Yeah, I'm getting lonesome," our heroine says. "Friends are everything."

"Promise you'll be there?" Major Sanchez Zamora asks.

"Yeah!" our heroine says. "It's more than a promise though. It's a dedication."

She hangs up.

Lieutenant Ortega Revelo looks at Major Sanchez Zamora who grins triumphantly. He starts the engine.

"Today even nature is at rest," he says as he slams his foot on the gas and speeds out of the car wash, leaving rubber...

...as our heroine's already waiting in front of Tusker's bed that he shares with the twins from the bar. Our heroine's dressed in a white Nike tracksuit. She looks cuddly as a teddy-bear and holds on to her precious bottle of Vitaminwater. A small duffel bag stands by her feet.

Tusker's loft in the posh neighborhood of Los Ceibos is tremendous. Everywhere gigantic photos of children.

African children.

Asian children.

Latino children.

Victims of war, famine, Aids, and the recent earthquake that hit Ecuador. Tusker has the talent to transfer the daily atrocities of humanity into something aesthetically magnetic. Something that he's learned from his parents. To move people's hearts with sadness.

¡Madre mia!

Our heroine looks at Tusker as he's waking up. Our heroine scares the hell out of him.

"Who the fuck are you?" he screams heartily.

"*Ecuador's got talent,*" our heroine says.

"What the...," Tusker continues.

"The agency sent me. I need pictures. For *Ecuador's got talent.* The TV show," our heroine says.

The twins wake up too. Everybody's naked.

"Well, fuck me," Tusker says.

"We did," the girls say. "A lot."

Our heroine ignores Tusker's props.

"The agency says you're good," our heroine says.

"I'm sorry?" Tusker says.

"The agency says you're the man," our heroine continues.

"Really?" Tusker says.

"The agency says you're flat broke," our heroine says.

She has Tusker's full attention now.

"The agency...," our heroine continues as Tusker interrupts her: "You bring cash?"

Our heroine smiles. Tusker rises.

"Where're my fucking pants?" he says. "What time is it?"

Our heroine spots Tusker's jeans on the floor. She picks them up and throws Tusker his denims. Tusker climbs over the girls. He maneuvers into his trousers. Tusker looks under the bed. He spots a bottle of tequila and goes for it. Tusker opens the bottle and offers it to our heroine. She shows him her bottle of Vitaminwater and smiles.

"My hangover has a hangover. Gotta take the edge off," he says and takes an impressive swig.

Tusker closes the bottle and throws it on the bed.

"Rise and shine, *niñas,* rise and shine," he says.

¿Niñas?

¡Niñas!

He spanks the girls on their bare asses. They scream and Tusker too finally wakes up. He extends his hand to our heroine. She accepts it.

"Name's Tusker," Tusker energetically introduces himself to our heroine.

"Tusker?" she asks.

"Just Tusker, yeah," he says. "Photographer per excellence. How do you do?"

Our heroine nods and smiles. Tusker is enticing, despite his foul demeanor.

"Welcome to my little paradise in the midst of such barbarism," he says.

Our heroine looks at the two girls who are still in bed.

"My self-appointed associates," Tusker says. "Cuba and Libre."

Tusker approaches our heroine and whispers in her ear: "To tell you the truth. I'm not sure when they snuck into my pad."

Tusker walks to the bed, lifts its frame and shakes it.

"Shoo, ladies. Daddy's got to make some money," he roars as he chases the girls out of his bed.

They look for their clothes and dress in a hurry.

Our heroine begins to study Tusker's photos. The melancholy of the pictures saddens her heart.

Tusker notices the effect his work has on his new client. He lights a smoke and goes to the bathroom as he says: "Few years ago. My life was a walking nervous breakdown. A real free-fall. I said to myself, Tusker, is your life about horror or is it about those few true seconds you have? Turned down many jobs and lots of money. Went to Africa instead. All over. Saw a lot of dead people. They were dead, you know. They had no place to go. Cause they were dead."

Tusker returns from the loo and approaches our heroine.

"And you know what I found out?" he asks her. "It's the same everywhere. Africa. South America. Ecuador. Those dead boys and girls. The earthquake. The world weeps at them being killed. The world feels bad about them. The rich need the poor more than the poor need the rich. Why? Cause those who have been subdued, right, need no longer be feared. Once I realized that, you know, I rejoined the modern world, before I started to do real harm. Sometimes you can't hide anything."

Our heroine reacts to Tusker's straightforward sobriety. Meanwhile the girls are dressed. They're waiting by the door. Tusker pulls his wallet out of his pocket. He opens it.

"Holy shit," he screams. "How the fuck did I spend so much fucking money?"

The girls look pissed. Our heroine pays them off. They leave.

"You're very generous," Tusker says. "Thank you. So, you want to win *Ecuador's got talent*?"

For some reason our heroine has doubts that she can continue with her mission.

"I should leave," she says and crosses to the door.

Tusker looks perplexed.

"Perhaps what you want is less than you could wish for," he says.

Our heroine turns around. She wants to give Tusker a second chance too.

"Surely there must be some people your heart likes to see," she says.

"You charge by the hour?" Tusker says. "Look, the universe doesn't have a desire to learn about us. The world's as good as its people."

"Something you don't like," our heroine says. "People."

"I love humankind," Tusker says. "I don't like humans though. I don't get along with people very well."

"So you don't care?" our heroine says.

"Everybody cares about something," Tusker answers as our heroine decides to continue with her initial plan.

"How much?" she asks.

"How much do I care?" Tusker asks.

"How much do you charge?" our heroine asks.

"The origin of every lie is a lack of respect," Tusker says as he approaches our heroine getting very close.

Our heroine trembles. Tusker whispers in her ear: "Fuck it. Let's get to work."

Tusker pats our heroine's cheek as he says: "Little *niña*."

¡Niña!

He turns around and grabs the bottle of tequila.

"Tequila makes you lose your mind and howl at the moon," he says. "You can change in the bathroom."

Tusker takes a huge tot from the bottle. Our heroine takes her bag and goes to the bathroom.

"So what do you do, *Ecuador's got talent*?" he asks.

Our heroine looks at Tusker. She's trying hard to be predominant. It's not effortless.

"There're things I do but do not mention," she says.

Tusker reacts to her words and then gets his camera equipment ready as he modifies the loft to a real photo studio until...

...our heroine strides out of the bathroom.

She's as cool and glossy as her blue sheath dress. All curves and emphatic sex appeal. Our heroine's radiating of self-confidence. The Vitaminwater bottle is still in her hand. Tusker's loading his Hasselblad 501CM. He remarks our heroine and is wowed by her appearance.

"You keep an archive, Tusker?" she asks.

Tusker looks at a metal cabinet.

"I sure do," he says. "That's where the ghosts gasp. Nothing ever dies on film."

Our heroine reacts as Tusker's getting ready to begin the session.

"Aspiration and personality come first before looks," he says as he drinks another shot of tequila.

"Only someone confident is someone beautiful," he continues. "You must have a great personality to make it to the major league."

Our heroine nods. She puts the Vitaminwater bottle on the floor. Tusker changes the lights to Cabaret atmosphere...

...and our heroine starts to dance.

She doesn't move much, though. Every ounce of power is reserved for filling Tusker's studio with the spine-tingling ballad of longed-for love.

Tusker photographs her. Our heroine begins to sing: "*Soñe ser tuyo y en mi efántenerte...*"

A cappella, unprompted, voce forte, her arms fling out to full wingspan, her head tosses back to bare her throat. As the ballad goes on, her voice swells and becomes an avalanche. It's a bravura performance, a sort of symphonic summoning of every woman who has been hurt before by injustice.

...meanwhile Major Sanchez Zamora and Lieutenant Ortega Revelo are driving to the next crime scene. Tusker's place. Traffic's a bitch though. They hardly move forward.

¡Este es Guayaquil!

Major Sanchez Zamora's face resembles someone who's about to crash his own surprise party. Lieutenant

Ortega Revelo looks like someone who's about to see a dentist as he picks up the two-way radio and begins to speak in it.

Major Sanchez Zamora's face now expresses exasperation while...

...Napomuk's packing a suitcase. He's very meticulous in doing so.

Napomuk puts the picture of his daughter on top of his clothes.

He counts his money. It's a few thousand US dollars. The savings of a lifetime.

Rabbi Napomuk Glass puts the money in his wallet as...

...our heroine ends her song, finishes belting. Tusker's totally out of breath. He's sweating bullets. Our heroine looks beatific, almost giddy.

"Wow," he says. "It's hard to find the words."

"Perhaps there's not much left to say. Look how free I am, look how free you could be," our heroine says as she picks up the Vitaminwater bottle.

"I'm Jorge Adalberto...," our heroine begins.

Tusker's not surprised at all. On the contrary.

"...Icaza Ortiz' wife. Of course you are. I never forget a face," he says as he points at the camera.

"If you're not in here, you don't exist," he says.

Our heroine's fuming. She's furious, raging, mad!

She opens the bottle as Tusker approaches our heroine. He's full of confidence and certainty. A cocky prick. Tusker caresses his beloved Hasselblad and says: "I'll make sure you'll be *Ecuador's got talent* new superstar. I'm connected. But you already know that. A year from now..."

Our heroine smiles and hands Tusker the Vitaminwater bottle.

"You're too kind. Did your husband appreciate you?" he says.

Our heroine looks at Tusker. He still hasn't accepted the bottle.

"Right," he says. "We should get to know each other. You do deserve some bang for your buck, *niña*."

¿Niña?

¡Niña!

Tusker takes the bottle, puts it in his mouth and...

...takes a tremendous gulp until...

...his eyes express dire pain and agony.

Tusker pulls the bottle out of his mouth and throws it against one of his Ecuador earthquake pictures.

The acid from the bottle splashes all over the photo. The image, a young boy badly injured, dissolves because of the chemical.

Tusker drops to his knees and gives in to the pain. His body goes into convulsions. His heart, lung, liver and kidneys are all under attack. Tusker's making involuntary crying sounds. Steam comes out of his mouth, nose, eyes and ears.

Just at the moment when it seems he cannot survive this, Tusker manages to enunciate one last phrase.

"You could've been a superstar," he says.

Our heroine looks at Tusker. Her eyes are empty.

"I have a nerve inside of me to do this. And I have no idea where it comes from, except that it might come from God. No one knows. But what I do know is this:

There are no second acts in American lives," she whispers as things are even getting worse.

Tusker continues to have grave seizures. The acid eats itself through his bones and skin as our heroine steps back and crosses to Tusker's archive.

She opens it and rummages through the photos. Eventually she finds what she's been looking for. Our heroine grabs a folder and sits down on the floor. She painstakingly opens it and looks at a set of photos. Our heroine closes her eyes and opens them again. Her face expresses horror, shock and speechlessness.

She silently begins to cry. Tears are streaming down her face and carry her...

...back five years earlier. Friday, April 1, 2011. We're in Ayampe. A small village at the Pacific Ocean. Our heroine's eyes are full of tears too. She's in a tastefully decorated bedroom dressed in a beautiful, white wedding gown.

A man in his early fifties is looking into a mirror. It's our heroine's husband: Jorge Adalberto Icaza Ortiz. He's wearing a black tuxedo and acts impatient with his bow tie.

Jorge Adalberto Icaza Ortiz is well-educated and soft-spoken. He's a unique blend of self-deprecation and dignity, his approachable elegance corresponds with his charisma without audacity. His old-world gentlemanliness is stunning. Everything about him seems authentic, genuine and true. Jorge Adalberto would make a conscious decision to run into a burning house in order to save lives. He's a man who places the safety of others above his own. Jorge Adalberto looks at our heroine. He notices her tears.

"*Niña,*" he says, "what's the matter?"

Our heroine dries her tears and gets up. She clears her throat and walks towards Jorge Adalberto. She reaches him and takes his handsome face into her hands.

"My love, how ugly you are. Why did I marry you?" she says.

Jorge Adalberto smiles kindly.

"Thank God, I'm not a poor man," he says as our heroine begins to work on his bow tie.

"We don't have to be rich," she says. "We've everything we need to be happy. We're so lucky. Do you know how lucky we are?"

Jorge Adalberto nods.

"Promise me something," our heroine continues.

"Anything," Jorge Adalberto says.

"I didn't marry you to eat lunch by myself. I didn't marry you to spend time by myself. I want to be with you. Always," our heroine declares as Jorge Adalberto smiles at her.

"Promised," he says.

Our heroine looks at him seriously.

"And I don't want to be a lonely old widow," she says.

"Don't worry, my love," he says, "I won't stick around longer than 75. Then you'll still be young, you'll still be beautiful, and some younger men will want to marry you for sure."

Jorge Adalberto laughs. The bow tie looks perfect now. Our heroine withdraws from Jorge Adalberto.

"I know, I'll have to share you," she says. "For a long time, men and women have demonstrated their optimism, dreaming of a new Ecuador. You listened, you heard. Now it's your time. I'll make sacrifices too. I have faith in you."

Jorge Adalberto reacts ambivalent.

"I wonder if maybe we're not monkeying around with things that are none of our business. I'm a scientist. I'm an astrophysicist. I study the stars. I study dark matter. I'm not meant for...," Jorge Adalberto says as our heroine puts her finger on his lips.

"That's why. That's why," she interrupts him. "The best leader will be the one who is ashamed to become a leader. Thousands of people all over the country have asked you to engage in this great fight. The people are on the march. We have assembled a Gideon's Army, small in number, powerful in conviction, ready for action. The people's peace will usher in the century of the common man. I never said this journey would be easy, and I won't promise that now. Yes, our path is harder, but it leads to a better place. Yes, our road is longer, but we travel it together. We don't turn back. We pull each other up. We draw strength from our victories. And we learn from our mistakes. But we keep our eyes fixed on that distant horizon knowing that providence is with us and that we are surely blessed to be citizens of the greatest nation on earth. Ecuador. You are their star. You're their dark matter!"

Jorge Adalberto smiles.

"Yes," he says, "everything's gonna be fine. As long as we've children. I'm hopeful because of you. My *niña.*"

Our heroine smiles.

"Just give me a child," Jorge Adalberto continues, "one child. That's all I want."

Our heroine caresses her belly.

"But I want more," she says, "I want at least five children. Or maybe three."

Our heroine takes Jorge Adalberto's hand. She carefully places it on her tummy. Jorge Adalberto looks at her and smiles. Our heroine beams back at the future father of her first child. Suddenly they hear a knock on the door. And a second one.

"I'll get it," Jorge Adalberto says as our heroine nods.

Our heroine looks at her belly in the mirror. She likes what she sees. Some moments pass. Jorge Adalberto does not return.

"Jorge Adalberto?" our heroine says.

No answer.

"Jorge Adalberto," our heroine says louder.

Nothing.

Our heroine glances at the door.

Her eyes express true distress...

...as they do now in the present.

Our heroine gets up and walks to the dead Tusker. She tosses the photos on the corpse as...

...Major Sanchez Zamora and Lieutenant Ortega Revelo bolt into the studio.

Major Sanchez Zamora has only eyes for our heroine. She stares at him. Her eyes reflect recognition. While Lieutenant Ortega Revelo inspects the disfigured Tusker.

"What a f- f- f-ine mess," he stutters.

He then picks up one of the photographs and...

"*Pa- pa- pa-tron*, is this you in...," he begins as quick as a flash Major Sanchez Zamora goes for his back up weapon.

He draws the NAA Mini Revolver from his ankle holster, points the gun at Lieutenant Ortega Revelo and...

...shoots his partner right between the eyes as he begins to sing *Adoracion* while tap dancing his way to our heroine: "*Soñé a mi lado para siempre verte, siendo tu único dueño, vida mia, soñé que eras mi diosa, mas la suerte nuevos tormentos para mi tenia.*"

When he reaches her, she's about to open her mouth and speak. Major Sanchez Zamora hits her with the revolver in the face. Our heroine goes to the ground. Hard.

"I would believe only in a God that knows how to dance. You've a problem with allowing someone to finish singing? *Calladita se ve más bonita*," Major Sanchez Zamora says.

Our heroine spits blood as Major Sanchez Zamora places the gun in her hand and fires a shot towards the door. He keeps the gun and continues singing *Adoracion* while collecting Tusker's photographs stuffing them into his coat pocket.

His sparkling eyes are just as dangerous as...

2.

...in the past as he draws across a tomato with his Swiss Army Knife.

"Elegant. Enduring. The blade is so familiar that we tend to overlook its technical refinement," Major Sanchez Zamora says. "With a blunt knife, you have to exert a large force to make a cut. But a sharp one can give us a surgeon's incision."

At first, Major Sanchez Zamora's knife senses the surface resistance, then a slight give as the blade eases through flesh to the board beneath, like a keel of a boat running into the sand.

"The blade, ladies and gentlemen," he continues, "was the breakthrough on which everything else is built."

Major Sanchez Zamora's in a stinted room at an unknown location.

Dazzling light.

Jorge Adalberto Icaza Ortiz is naked.

His body shows signs of severe torture.

His hands are shackled behind him.

He's suspended by his wrists from a hook in the ceiling.

Wham!

Suddenly there's a crackling and splintering in his shoulders. It's if he's falling into a void and hangs there by his dislocated arms which are torn high from behind and are now twisted over his head.

"A man,", Major Sanchez Zamora says, "a man, to be greatly good, must imagine intensely and comprehensively; he must put himself in the place of another and many others; the pains and pleasures of his species must become his own. The great instrument of moral goods is in the imagination."

Cabby Erick Andres Pena Segale aka Antonio de la Cruz stands by the door.

Deputy Mayor Ilcamaria Fiorela von Buchwald leans against a wall next to radio personality Alejandro Mateo Torres Estrada fixing his hair.

Meanwhile Tusker's taking pictures of *Señor* Ricardo Miguel Santos Calderon who is armed with a horsewhip with which he beats Jorge Adalberto.

Jorge Adalberto screams in agony and pain as Major Sanchez Zamora's eating a slice of tomato. He closes his Swiss Army Knife.

"In every real man a child is hidden that wants to play," he says.

"This man has what?" he then asks the others. "This man has everything. Except the faintest idea of what we're about to do to him."

The group reacts as *Señor* Santos Calderon hits Jorge Adalberto again.

Jorge Adalberto screams.

"Didn't he watch the news?" *Señor* Santos Calderon asks cynically.

"What news?" von Buchwald laughs.

"Who's this guy anyway?" Alejandro Mateo Torres Estrada asks. "He's never been on my show."

Tusker keeps on photographing.

"No faces, you hear!" *Señor* Santos Calderon demands as Tusker secretly continues photographing their faces too, just in case. He says: "It's all for the history books. Put a nice face to the bad times."

"Let me tell you who this man is," Major Sanchez Zamora says to Alejandro Mateo Torres Estrada. "He's a man of ideas. Educated. Independent. Wealthy. A man of conviction. A fool with faith. And reason. But God is dead. God remains dead. And this man has killed him."

Alejandro Mateo Torres Estrada nods.

"You know, ladies and gentlemen," Major Sanchez Zamora continues, "you know, what really disappoints me?"

The group reacts.

"The level of ignorance that surrounds people like him. You see, to be a good man, one must become independent of all external signs of success," Major Sanchez Zamora says.

He slowly moves towards Jorge Adalberto as *Señor* Santos Calderon moves away from him offering the horsewhip to Major Sanchez Zamora who ignores the gesture and smiles.

He looks down at Jorge Adalberto who's trembling.

"Please," he says, "I'm begging you, please!"

"Don't worry," Major Sanchez Zamora whispers, "everybody's behind you on this one. And remember, this isn't a dream. This is really happening."

"Tell me something I don't know," he then continues. "Who are your friends? I want a list. Who is still working on your behalf? Who is shaping your policy in our beloved Ecuador?"

"Please," Jorge Adalberto begs, "let me go home. My wife's waiting. She'll be worried. It's my wedding day."

"Don't mess up an apology with an excuse, my friend," Major Sanchez Zamora says. "Electrify me with a bold decision. Bold decisions make history. Not heroism. It's hard to be a hero without a war. Heroes need battles and bombs and bullets in order to be heroic. That's why I'm suspicious of the military. They're always so narrow in their appraisal of everything. They see everything in military terms. Nothing could possibly be worse than that. You see, I've treated many hundreds of men like you. Among those in the second half of life - that is to say, over 35 - there has not been one whose problem in the last resort was not that of finding a religious outlook on life. Name the names."

Jorge Adalberto keeps silent and cries.

"Not many people handle gratitude very well, I'm afraid," Major Sanchez Zamora continues as he grabs Jorge Adalberto's head and yells: "Tell the truth, and shame the devil!"

Jorge Adalberto has no strength left.

He can't respond.

The group reacts.

"I don't want to deal with these piddling little things, "von Buchwald says. "We must deal with the main issue."

"I think, you can stop now," Alejandro Mateo Torres Estrada says to Major Sanchez Zamora. "Don't you see what you've done?"

"Oh, my God, what was I considering?" von Buchwald says as Major Sanchez Zamora looks at everybody.

¡Por dios!

He's far from being done with Jorge Adalberto. Major Sanchez Zamora is just getting started. He gets significantly close to his Jorge Adalberto's face, wearing his finest MD expression.

"Forgive me," he says, "I'm just playing my part. And I do have a stubborn streak in me."

Major Sanchez Zamora opens his Swiss Army Knife again and...

...looks at Jorge Adalberto's genitals.

"It is a fact that cannot be denied, the wickedness of others becomes our own wickedness because it kindles something evil in our hearts. For to kill, ladies and gentlemen," he says, "is the great law set by nature in the heart of existence. There's nothing more beautiful and honorable than killing. There's a gap between what they know and what they believe. Let's make sure this gap persists."

Major Sanchez Zamora cuts off Jorge Adalberto's private parts and stuffs them into his victim's mouth. The others react to Jorge Adalberto who's screaming like a pig being slaughtered.

"And we call ourselves the human race," Alejandro Mateo Torres Estrada says as Jorge Adalberto slowly suffocates and bleeds to death.

"Now we're all sons-of-bitches," von Buchwald says.

"We may be humans, but we're still animals," Tusker says.

"When your time's up, it's up," Erick Andres Pena Segale aka Antonio de la Cruz says.

Major Sanchez Zamora looks at his audience.

"*Que bonito es ver llover y no mojarse.* I'm a pure-blooded Ecuadorian nobleman without a single drop of bad blood. Certainly not his blood. Welcome to our little reunion. Class of 1986. What? You don't like final solutions?" he says as our heroine...

...paces in front of her house. She's still wearing her wedding dress. She's alone. It's the time of darkness between one day and the next. The time of day when no light from the sun can be seen. The time from dusk to dawn.

A van appears in the distance and approaches. Eventually it stops in front of our heroine. The sliding door opens. Alejandro Mateo Torres Estrada and *Señor* Santos Calderon throw Jorge Adalberto out of the van.

The dead body ends up right in front of our heroine. She goes down on her knees.

Our heroine looks at her husband and then into the van. She sees Major Sanchez Zamora, Deputy Mayor von Buchwald, radio personality Alejandro Mateo Torres Estrada, businessman *Señor* Santos Calderon, driver Pena Segale aka Antonio de la Cruz and Tusker who is still taking photos.

One of them screams: "Good luck, *niña*!"

The sliding door closes.

The van hauls off as...

...a few minutes later our heroine runs across Ayampe's magnificent beach. Her dress is covered with blood, dirt and water. Our heroine falls and gets up again. She continues to run. The rolling surf rushes forward and reaches the beach. It splashes against the shore. Our heroine stops. Like life stops. Her life. She's waiting for the next rolling wave to carry her out. She just doesn't care for being on land any longer. She wants to finish her life. She's alone with nature. And nature leaves her alone. She looks into the sky. It's a starry night. Even the moon is visible. Our heroine touches her belly. Water tickles her barefoot little feet. She feels life. Jorge Adalberto's life. And her life.

She will turn herself into events, keeps shedding old skins. Her initial obsession with masquerade predicts the double lives we all live now, our simultaneous existences as living, breathing people and disembodied avatars.

"Stars don't care what you wish for. Or do they?" she says to herself knowing that she will do the killings herself. In the first place...

...Major Sanchez Zamora who approaches her now in the present.

"Endurance is what?" he says. "It's everything, *niña*. It's a virtue. Tenderness beyond a certain point just sissy."

"How come you're so ugly," our heroine says as Major Sanchez Zamora is about to shoot her.

Right at this very moment several policeman bolt into the studio. They react to the dead Tusker and the equally dead Lieutenant Ortega Revelo. Major Sanchez Zamora slowly walks to the cops. He appears to be shaken to the core.

"Shot Gino in cold blood," he says.

He hands the gun to his colleague and wipes a tear off his face. The cop nods and pats Major Sanchez Zamora's shoulder.

"I know how you feel, Major," the cop says.

"Yes," Major Sanchez Zamora answers, "he was like a son to me."

"And you like a father to him," the cop says. "I wish one day I'll be like you."

"You will be, my friend, you will be," Major Sanchez Zamora smiles.

"Book her," the cop orders and points at our heroine.

"Didn't you forget something?" Major Sanchez Zamora asks.

The cop reacts.

"Read her rights. After all, we're a democracy," Major Sanchez Zamora says.

"Of course," the cop says. "I'm sorry, Major."

Major Sanchez Zamora and our heroine look at each other. Suddenly he notices a spider on the floor. It's a Black Widow.

Delightfully Major Sanchez Zamora crushes the insect with his foot.

Part Three

1.

Thursday afternoon, April 28, 2016. Nepomuk's seated in front of a desk at Amazing Tours, a travel agency at the Galeria Millenium Planta Baja Local. A television set in hanging from the ceiling. Across from Nepomuk sits a young, female clerk.

"It's always been my dream to see Germany," she says.

"Really?" Nepomuk answers.

"And the food...," the woman continues.

"Of course," Nepomuk nods.

"The people must be so nice," she says.

"Are they?" Nepomuk asks.

"Round-trip to Germany...," the agent begins.

"One-way ticket will do," Nepomuk interrupts her.

"Oh," she says.

"And I'll pay cash," Nepomuk adds.

"Cash?" the woman asks.

"*Genau*," Nepomuk finishes the conversation.

The clerk reacts puzzled but obliges.

"All right," she says, turns around and checks her computer for flight availability.

Suddenly Breaking News on TC Televisión. Footage on our heroine's arrest.

"Turn it up!" Nepomuk orders.

Done.

"An unidentified woman has been arrested for multiple homicide. According to police sources," reporter Debbie Benites says as the camera shows Major Sanchez Zamora's face, "the numbers of dead vary. The case is one of the most severe and gruesome in Guayaquil's history."

"We never lost sight of the bigger picture," Major Sanchez Zamora says and looks directly into the camera. "I need to make clear that any death is deeply regrettable."

The clerk turns around to Nepomuk. She'd been watching the news too.

"This horrible woman. Our beloved city," she says and notices that Nepomuk...

...is gone.

Thursday evening, April 28, 2016. Ecuador's largest prison: Guayaquil's Litoral. A few thousand men. Hundreds of women. Dozens of children. Designed to hold 600 inmates. A filthy place, infested with roaches, rats the size of rabbits. Bribes buy bed, food, lawyers. The convicts call themselves *las muertas invidas* - the living dead.

Our heroine sits in the tailor shop. She's trying on her pink prison pantsuit. Other female detainees stare at her.

"There's no hurry," one says. "Time means nothing. Why're you here?"

"Love," our heroine answers.

The women laugh.

"She speaks of love," another one says. "He's probably wounded her heart forever."

They laugh again.

"There're only two things wrong with men: too big or too small," the first one says as the others applaud her.

"You'll get used to us," a third one says to our heroine.

"What brings you here, besides love? Envy? Spite? Secretiveness? Resentment? Bigotry? Long-suffering? Frigidity? Malice? Sullenness? Churlishness? Hypocrisy? Niggardliness? Self-pity? Vindictiveness? Pettiness? Procrastination? Sloth? Or was it perhaps jealousy?" the chorus of woman asks.

"No, it was love," our heroine says calmly.

"Look, *niña*," one woman says, "you're at the right place. Sharing and bearing it."

A jailor enters the shop.

"Got a visitor," he says to our heroine who's now dressed in her pink suit, approaching the jailor.

"Hey, *niña*," one of the inmates shouts as our heroine turns around.

!Niña!

"I carry death between my breasts. Sometimes I take it out and talk to it. I say, hello, baby, how ya doing? When you coming for me? I'll be ready," the woman shouts as our heroine exits the tailor shop.

A razor blade is gone, and Nepomuk...

...has arrived in the prison reception. A jailor eyes him suspiciously.

"Your daughter?" he asks.

"Yes, my daughter. I'm here to see my daughter. She's my daughter," Nepomuk says.

The jailor nods and begins to grin wickedly.

Nepomuk understands but also feels that there's not much time left. He needs to play the game. Nepomuk takes out his wallet.

"All right, *Kollege*," he says, "you wanna know who I am? I'm a Christ-killing, world-dominating, media-controlling kike. How much?"

At the same time our heroine steps into a dark cell. The jailor stays outside and locks the door. Someone switches the lights on, and a heavily decorated visitor stands there. It's Major Sanchez Zamora who wears his new uniform: General Supervisor. Highest rank at the Policia Nacional del Ecuador. General Supervisor Sanchez Zamora smiles and opens his arms.

"A bit quick, but well deserved. Don't you think, *niña*?" he says.

¡Niña!

General Supervisor Sanchez Zamora's in a great mood.

"*Niña*," he says, "if you ever pray, pray for me now. I don't know whether you ever had a load of hay fall on you, but when 'they' told me what 'they' wanted me to be, I felt like the moon, the stars and all the planets had fallen on me. I've got the most terribly responsible job a man ever had, and I couldn't give a rat's tutu about what you did. Why? Cause when you're dead you're dead. That's it. Let us beware of saying that death is the opposite of life. The living being is only a species of the dead, and a very rare species. And trust me, feminism, feminism is my fight. In fact, until more men get involved in this fight, nothing will change at all. You might have a country of enlightened women ready to kick some ass and change things, but the very people who run this world will just be standing there with their arms crossed, and I've kicked more ass than you've sat on. My idea of feminism is what? Self-determination, and it's very open-ended. Every woman has the right to become herself, and do whatever she needs to do. Nobody likes a turncoat. I hear ya, *niña.* Today I love myself as I love my God. Who could charge me with a sin today? I know only sins against my God. But who knows my God? I requested that my tombstone reads: *feo, fuerte y formal.* "

Our heroine approaches General Supervisor Sanchez Zamora.

"People seldom do what they believe in," he continues. "They do what is convenient, then repent. Once a woman has forgiven her man, she must not reheat his sins for breakfast. The difference between winners and losers is that winners do what losers don't wanna do. But just because I accept you as you are does not mean that I've given up all hope of your improvement. Blessed are the forgetful, for they get the better even of their blunders. My advice to women is what? To raise more hell and less dahlias. Don't get me wrong. I don't preclude myself from being enthusiastic about what I do. I work very hard - if you can call it work. I put everything I've got in. Invest myself into all. I always want it to work out well for everyone concerned. But I find in the end, no one gives a shit about anything. Oh, hell. I was born at the wrong time. Right after independence. That was the time. The railroad promised. The law about to settle into place. If you have cattle, someone will steal them. If you have a house, someone will burn it. There may be a sheriff or a marshal, a good man perhaps, but a weak one. But, you know, how could there be shoot-ups if there was no one to do the shooting? What, then, am I, this new man? That strange mixture of blood and bones, which you find in no other country. I act upon new principles? It's good I'm the fucking sheriff of this fucking lawless piece-of-shit town. Well, it is impossible to suffer without making someone pay for it. Every complaint already contains revenge. I must therefore entertain new ideas and form new opinions. I hold it that a little rebellion now and then is a good thing, and as necessary in the political world as storms are in the physical. You and I, we're what? Two peas in a pot. Not duped by morality. The future influences the present just as much as the past. These days, women are better hung than men. *El que va para Quito pierde su banquito.*"

Our heroine has reached General Supervisor Sanchez Zamora. She now stands directly in front of him.

"Any regrets?" she asks.

"Not the slightest," General Supervisor Sanchez Zamora answers. "Not the slightest in the world. Sitting forward elbows on knees, oh what a luck to able to crap, *niña.*"

¡Niña!

"I wish you to know that you've been the last nightmare of my soul. Oops. That was rude," our heroine says. "But you know, I've been naughty too. You know what naughty girls need. And I know you want release. Come to visit. *Quien anda con lobos a aullar aprende.*"

She unbuttons the top of her pantsuit and goes for his groin.

"Do not, above all, confound me with what I'm not. That would go against elementary logic," General Supervisor Sanchez Zamora warns her as he lifts his hand and stops her from going any further.

General Supervisor Sanchez Zamora gives our heroine his be-all and end-all MD look.

"You chocolatecoated Satan sandwich," he says. "I felt a breeze below my waist and realized that my fly was open, wasn't it? You see, there's plenty of fire down below. But you'd never be able to satisfy me. A soft cock never lies. Agh! Fuck diabetes and stroke. How about a plate of black forest chocolate cake?"

¡Què cabrón. El maricòn!

"Be in the moment. I'm a lot calmer now. Why don't you try and make a man of me?" our heroine asks as suddenly someone's opening the door and General Supervisor Sanchez Zamora's distracted for a second.

Our heroine seizes the moment.

The razor blade materializes between her teeth and like an ozelot she leaps at General Supervisor Sanchez Zamora and slits his fucking throat.

General Supervisor Sanchez Zamora's blood splutters everywhere. He goes to the ground and - drowns in his blood. The cell door opens.

Nepomuk and a jailor enter. The jailor looks at General Supervisor Sanchez Zamora in his puddle of blood. He's in total shock and runs away.

Nepomuk looks at our heroine who's cleaning her mouth.

"Is it over?" he asks.

Our heroine nods as Nepomuk looks at General Supervisor Sanchez Zamora.

"Masel tov, motherfucker," he says. "And now?"

Our heroine goes for the Little Joe Five Shot Revolver, which is embedded in General Supervisor Sanchez Zamora's belt buckle holder. She releases the gun and points it at Nepomuk's head as she pushes him out of the cell taking him as her hostage.

They exit the cell...

...and arrive in the prison corridor.

"Out of the fucking way!" our heroine screams at two jailors who block their way. "Or I'll kill the fucking Jew. I'll blow his fucking brains out!"

The jailors let them pass and...

...they eventually arrive outside of *Litoral* where Nepomuk leads them to his car, a black 1979 Mercedes 240 D. Nepomuk gets behind the wheel.

Our heroine runs around the car to the passenger's side and...

...has an accident.

She trips and falls so ill-fated that she shoots herself in the lower body. Our heroine manages, however, to get into the car.

"You okay?" Nepomuk asks.

"Go!" she orders.

Nepomuk presses the foot on the gas and speeds away.

He doesn't notice that our heroine is severely injured and drives into the night until...

...they arrive at the Pacific Ocean. It's Friday morning, April 29, 2016. Ayampe. A small village. Our heroine's village. The same place where she wanted to take her life five years ago.

Our heroine and Nepomuk glance outside. The eye-filling sea before them throws out a softness and a warmth that is breathless. Nepomuk looks at our heroine. She's as pale as a ghost. Nepomuk finally notices her wound.

"We've got to get you to a hospital," he says.

Our heroine smiles.

"You've got me home, Nepo," she says. "Look at this."

Nepomuk reacts anxious and afraid.

"Listen...," he begins.

"No, Nepo," she interrupts him, "you listen. There's a bridge I want you to cross."

Nepomuk nods.

"That's not what I'm talking about. You're a man of many talents," she says. "There's someone who needs you, someone who never had a balloon burst. Who never fell off a bike and skinned a knee. Someone you need to force to conjugate and to keep quiet during lunch and dinner. This person, I hope, will learn how it feels like to have a quarter roll with weary deliberation down a grate. What luck."

Nepomuk doesn't understand.

"I explained everything," our heroine says. "In a letter. It's in your house. Come here."

Nepomuk moves closer to our heroine. She whispers something in his ear. Nepomuk withdraws.

"That's the most beautiful name I've ever heard," he says. "Very nice to meet you."

"Pleasure's all mine," our heroine says. "Look at your face. It's, perhaps, the very presence of God."

Our heroine begins to cough.

"Nepo," she says.

"Yes," he answers.

"I think this is my swan song. Thank you," she says as she takes Nepomuk's hand and looks outside.

Nepomuk follows suit as the sun slowly rises.

"Don’t worry, love," our heroine sighs. "I’m just shape-shifting again."

A few weeks before Christmas Nepomuk finds himself at the Hacienda de Esperanza at the foot of the snow covered Cayambe volcano. It's Saturday, December 10, 2016.

He sits across Sandra Jaeger who runs the orphanage. She glances through many documents. A Christmas tree stands in the corner.

"That's, well," she begins, "quite the adventure you've had."

"Life's full of surprises," Nepomuk answers.

"I know it's been a long process," she continues, "but we've had to make sure that... How old are you?"

"Well, let's just say I'm not greedy anymore," Nepomuk says.

Mrs. Jaeger reacts.

"Right," she says. "Retirement?"

"You're talking about death?" Nepomuk asks. "Not yet. Not yet."

Mrs. Jaeger smiles and asks: "So who are you, Mr. Glass?"

"Who I am?" Nepomuk asks back. "I am astonished, disappointed, pleased with myself. I am distressed, depressed, rapturous. I am all these things at once, and cannot add up the sum. I am incapable of determining ultimate worth or worthlessness. I have no judgement about myself and my life. There is nothing I am quite sure about. I have no definite convictions - not about anything, really. I know only that I was born and exist, and it seems to me that I have been carried along. I exist on the foundation or something I don't know. In spite of all uncertainties, I feel a solidity underlying all existence and a continuity in my mode of being a Mensch."

"Right," Mrs. Jaeger says, "The child's mother..."

"Like dark matter," Nepomuk says, "she was vitally important, but easy to overlook."

Only a few moments later Nepomuk faces a pretty 4-year-old girl sitting on a bench. A small suitcase rests next to her. She's holding on tight to a stuffed teddy bear.

"Does your house have a chimney?" the girl asks seriously.

Nepomuk reacts.

"No," he says. "Why?"

"How will Santa get into your house if you don't have a chimney?", the girl asks even more earnestly.

Santa Claus? Christmas? Not really Nepomuk's cup of tea. But once again Nepomuk adapts himself to the circumstances of his life.

"He has a magic key," Nepomuk says as our heroine's daughter smiles.

She gets up and hands him the suitcase.

"I'm Daniela Helena Icaza Ortiz," she says.

"I know," Nepomuk says. "I'm rabbi Nepomuk Glass. Call me Nepo. Shalom."

"Shalom," Daniela Helena Icaza Ortiz repeats as they begin walking down the corridor.

Nepomuk's legs hurt, of course. He's still a slow walker. But he never walks back.

"What happened to your legs?" Daniela Helena Icaza Ortiz asks.

"Oh, that's a long story," Nepomuk answers as Daniela Helena Icaza Ortiz takes his hand and says: "I like long stories."

"Good," rabbi Nepomuk Glass answers. "We've all the time in the world."

Epilogue

Hans Lipschis (born November 7, 1919) is a former member of the Waffen-SS who worked at Auschwitz during World War II. The Simon Wiesenthal Center alleges that he was a guard and listed him in fourth place on their most wanted list. He claims that although he worked at the concentration camp, he was only a cook. He was fund to be unfit for trial. Lipschis lives in the southwestern German town of Aalen.

Table of Contents

europabuch